The Legacy of Eagle Creek

Bobbie Shafer

Publishers Note:

This is a work of fiction. All names, characters, places, and events are the work of the author's imagination. Any resemblance to real persons, places, or events is coincidental.

Cover Art: Justin James
www.darempiremedia.com

DWB PUBLISHING
www.dancingwithbearpublishing.com

This book is dedicated to my husband Gordon, for his faith in me; my children, Connie, Kim, Cary, and Kelly for their support and help with my books; for Beverly, Jyll, Melanie, and Peggy at Troup Library for all their help, and to all my readers. Last, but not least, to Marie McGaha, for her hard work in editing my story. Without their support and dedication, I would be lost.

~ One ~
Impossible Dream

The overloaded wagon groaned when Clayton Wilkins pulled the reins sharply to the left and guided the straining horses off the main road onto the private driveway. His oldest daughter, Sarah, sat next to him, clutching her late mother's hand-painted lamp tightly in both hands. The wagon swayed to the right, and Sarah tried to stay balanced when the wagon bounced over the entrance.

Clayton glanced over his shoulder at the other passengers. His two youngest children, Mary and Clay Jr., and his father- and mother-in-law, Joseph and Irene Martin, sat on crates in the wagon bed between boxes of their belongings, and they all held on tightly to the side rails.

Clayton flicked the reins, encouraging the horses to continue up the private roadway to their new, never-before-seen home. The wagon wheels crunched over small, white gravel bearded with weeds and grass, poking up here and there. After angling around a wide curve through tall, swaying cedar trees, the house came into sight. Clayton pulled the horses to a complete stop, and stared.

The house on the hill was a magnificent, enormous two-storied, white plantation-style creation, with a porch on the first floor that circled the front, sides and back. The second story had a balcony that mirrored the one below, and gables with curtained windows jutted out from the attic area, suggesting living space available there. Several weather-worn rocking chairs were scattered along the porch, accompanied by a few small side tables.

The overgrown shrubbery, weed-filled flower beds, and the untamed Jasmine vines that struggled up every post and shutter, could not diminish the beauty of Eagle Creek Manor.

"Papa, you must have made a wrong turn somewhere. This can't be the right house," Sarah said, her eyes wide with wonder.

Clayton remembered the day he announced to Sarah, and her siblings, that he put in a silent bid on an unseen house with property, in the next county. By his daughter's reaction, he knew she feared the worst. Now he wondered if she could be right. His four hundred dollar bid would certainly not have bought this incredibly beautiful mansion, garden, and rolling meadow. Maybe Fate was being cruel, taunting them with grandeur they could never afford.

Mentally, Clayton agreed with Sarah's assessment. When he discovered a few days ago he, and his crew, no longer had a job at the cotton mill due to a buy-out, Clayton took the chance of his lifetime. He was expecting a small two-story cabin, certainly not this spectacular home.

He reached under the seat and retrieved a package stored there earlier. Pulling out the brown folder, he untied and shuffled through a stack of papers, reading each one carefully before moving on to the next.

Clayton looked up with a wide grin, and held out one of the papers to Sarah.

"No, Miss Wilkins, there is no mistake. It says right here in black and white, Eagle Creek Farm, two-story structure, with seven hundred and sixty attached acres. There is a cold creek from the mountain, two ponds, several outbuildings, a barn, stable, and spring-fed well."

He looked at his children's astonished faces, picked up the reins, and clucked his tongue at the horses. The wagon moved slowly up to the front of the house, and halted by the steps of the wide porch. The roof of the porch provided the floor to the covered balcony of the second floor, which ran around the same three sides.

Mary and Little Clay bounded out of the wagon, while Joseph helped his wife, Irene, down from the back. Clayton leaped to the ground and held his arms out to Sarah. She stepped onto the wheel, still clutching the lamp, and he swung her to the ground. They walked up the wide porch steps to the front double doors with a stained glass inlay of a large, golden eagle with a crystal eye.

Clayton shoved his hand into his pocket and dug for the key William Gaines, the banker in Sycamore Grove, gave him. Mr. Gaines' niece, Lillian Anderson, volunteered to guide Clayton to the recently acquired property, and rode up on her horse

Lillian went to the door, and turned toward Clayton and his family. She looked down at her split skirt and masculine shirt, and smiled ruefully.

"I know you nice people must think I dress outrageously, and am forward and pushy. You're right, I do and I am. I love the outdoors and ride every day. I have found that riding in a full skirt, with my waist cinched up so tight I can hardly breathe, is unacceptable. I dress comfortably. Life is too short not to enjoy it thoroughly, and that's just what I plan to do."

Clayton smiled but he couldn't find the words to respond. Irene rescued him by stepping forward and putting her arm around Lillian Anderson.

"I don't ride very often anymore, but I can definitely see the outfit you have on is certainly more appropriate for riding than a full skirt with lots of petticoats. I also agree that corsets are most uncomfortable, and wouldn't be something you would want to ride in.

"Life is indeed short. We know that all too well. Don't apologize for being you. Honesty is a refreshing attribute, and it suits you well. Don't change for anyone." She gave Lillian a quick hug and wide smile.

Sarah shook her head worriedly. "Papa, this is plain old spooky. This house must have cost a fortune to build, especially way out here, not to mention the barn and... well, this just can't be right. Who in their right mind would not scoop up this house the moment it came on the market?

"Four hundred dollars wouldn't buy this beautiful door." She peered through one of the glass panels that graced either side of the door.

Lillian stepped up beside Clayton and shyly touched his arm. "Mister Wilkins, do you mind if I come inside with you and your family? Although I have ridden through this property all my life, I've never had the opportunity to see the inside, and I'm about to explode with curiosity."

"Why, certainly Miss Anderson. That's the least we can do in exchange for your guiding us out here," Clayton said.

"Thank you. You're very kind."

Sarah went to one of the large windows and peered through, shading her eyes with her cupped hand.

"Oh, Papa," she cried out loudly.

Stepping back quickly, she crossed her arms

over her chest. Irene reached out and grabbed Sarah's arm, pulling her back.

"What is it, dear? What did you see?" she asked in alarm.

"Papa Joe, you better get the gun," Clayton said sharply.

"Don't bother," Lillian said, her eyes narrowing. "I've got mine."

Clayton turned to see her holding a pistol pointed at the door.

"No, no, you don't need the gun. It's just that, that—there's furniture in there," Sarah gasped.

"Tarnation, Sarah Susannah Wilkins," her grandfather said. "You scared the life clean outta us—over a chair."

Lillian laughed softly and slid her handgun back in its holster at her side. She quickly pulled her jacket together, hiding the gun from view. When she looked up, the entire family was staring at her.

"I didn't mean to frighten you," she said. "Nearly everyone around here carries a gun. Well," she paused, "nearly everyone. You never know when you might run into a snake, coyote, wolf, or something worse."

Clayton coughed, breaking the silence following Lillian's explanation.

"Let's go in and see this frightening furniture. Do you think I should get a stick in case we're attacked by a lamp or, heaven forbid, a sofa or table?" His shoulders shook with silent laughter.

"You may all think this quite funny, but I tell you that this house and land selling for a few hundred dollars worries me, and it should worry you," Sarah said. "When you put in the bid back home, did the banker mention why it hasn't sold before?" Susan looked hard at her father, and then at Lillian.

Clayton thought for a moment. "He did say a few others put in offers for the place but I can't recall if he said why it hadn't sold. Maybe it's haunted." He slapped his knee and guffawed. He turned to Lillian. "It isn't haunted, is it?"

Lillian just smiled.

"Honey," Irene said gently, and rested her hand on Sarah's shoulder. "Whoever built this house way out here obviously wanted privacy and seclusion. I imagine most wealthy people want a house they can show off. I can't see too many fancy wives of high society living way out here where their belongings couldn't be admired or envied. They'd miss too many tea parties and fancy balls."

Sarah smiled at her grandmother. "I never thought about that. I guess Sycamore Grove isn't exactly the hub of society."

"No, it isn't very big but it is a lovely little town. I think we have everything you folks might need," Lillian said, her voice tinged with a defensive note.

"Yes, Miss Anderson's right. I think it has all that we need," Clayton agreed. "I saw a bank, general store, blacksmith shop, dress shop, school, and a small sawmill. I'm sure there are several other businesses that we didn't see. We'll drive down in a day or so, and see it all up close. Whatever my family needs, I'll make sure you have it, even if I have to drive all the way to Dawson City to get it. You will not do without, I promise." He pulled Sarah close and kissed her forehead.

Clayton opened his hand, tossed the key in the air, grinned, caught in, and poked it into the keyhole and twisted. There was a loud click, and with a turn of the doorknob, the beautiful front door swung open.

Before anyone could enter, a loud clatter from the side yard snatched their attention away from the house.

"Papa, Sarah, y'all come see," Little Clay called from the corner of the porch. "There's chickens running loose in the back, and Mary says she heard a dog barking in the woods."

"Clay Junior, you and Mary come over here this instant. I don't want you wandering around out there all alone," Sarah said firmly. "And stay away from any dog you see. It's probably wild, vicious, and may have rabies."

"Aw, Sarah," Clay Jr. whined.

"Do what your sister says, Son," Papa Joe advised. "Things go a lot smoother down the road when the womenfolk are happy." He grinned. "Besides, don't you want to pick out your very own room?"

"Oh, yeah, I almost forgot about that." He pretended to hit the invisible pony he was riding. "Giddyup boy, we gotta find us a good room. Mary," he yelled. "Let's go pick out a room. Don't you wanna pick one out, Sarah?"

Mary raced over, leaped onto the porch, and bounded up the stairs with her brother, both shrieking and laughing. Even Sarah, despite all her misgivings, smiled. She nodded to her father, went inside, and rushed up the stairs after her siblings to select her own room.

"Madam. Sir. Honored guest. Shall we take the royal tour?" Clayton swept his arm wide and bent in a low bow. "Lord and ladies, I beg your attendance."

Once inside, the group was again dumbfounded. It seemed that being astonished by this house was an ongoing emotion.

Twin staircases ran upstairs from both sides of the first floor hall, and the second floor hallway ran all around the house, and looked down on the entrance. A large crystal chandelier hung from the second floor ceiling, to below the second floor railing. A chain attached to the wall on the second floor draped down, so the chandelier could be lowered to the first floor in order to light the dozens of candles adorning it.

The wallpaper was a soft cream color with golden cream vertical stripes that seemed to glow in the soft light, filtering in through the windows.

After recovering from the beauty of the hallway, Clayton slid open two doors to his right.

"This, I take it, is the living room, or parlor, or sitting room, or something or other." He crossed the room, and slid open another set of doors to the adjoining room. "This is obviously the library," he said. He paused to look at the floor-to-ceiling shelves filled with books.

"Oh, Clayton, look at all these books. There must be hundreds of them. If Susan were only..." Irene paused and covered her mouth.

Clayton closed his eyes and silently agreed with his mother-in-law. His beloved wife loved books, and read the same battered ones over and over again. Now there were more books than she could read in a lifetime, although she wasn't here to read them.

Papa Joe crossed the room, and opened the door to what looked like an office or study. Irene walked back to the entrance hall, and crossed to the room opposite. There, she discovered the actual parlor, a formal dining room, serving room, and stepping down a small staircase from the serving room, she stood in the kitchen of every woman's dream.

Sarah danced lightly down the staircase, her heart lighter now that she had seen the magnificent home filled with lovely furniture, and the beautiful land that surrounded it. She heard her grandmother talking to Lillian, and followed the sound of their voices through the dining room, into the kitchen.

"Sarah, you must look at this." Irene smiled and wiggled her finger toward her granddaughter, beckoning her to join them.

The kitchen was enormous. A gigantic fireplace covered one entire wall, with a six burner woodstove against the other wall, and an additional smaller one beside it. In the center of the room sat an over-sized table. Two smaller rooms off the kitchen were filled with canned goods, and glass jars containing fruits and vegetables. Another door led down to the basement that none of the women wished to explore at the moment.

A large windowed door led out to a lovely herb garden, filled with overflowing urns of mint, rosemary, dill, and several unknown plants. Here and there, the small garden was decorated with several delicate garden statues. By a small pool, a figure of King Neptune stood with his three-pronged staff. At the edge of the water was a ring of sea horses.

A tiny bench sat in the center, where three mermaids combed their hair. Two small, graceful dolphins rose from the far side, and in the center, stood a large ornate fountain, designed to overflow into the lily-filled pool. There were several benches on the grassy area surrounded by wild flowers, and peeking from clumps of herbs, were stone turtles, crabs and other sea creatures.

"It's hard to believe that a man created this wonderful kitchen and that exquisite garden. It is a little odd that with the drive grown over, and the front yard so full of weeds, this garden is in fairly good shape.

"I am surprised that it looks so good. Whoever weeded it last really made sure it wouldn't grow back quickly. Of course, that's the answer. It probably was well-weeded, and hasn't grown back. This whole house echoes a woman's touch," Irene said softly.

"Well," Sarah mused, "maybe he did have a woman in mind when he built this but it just didn't work out. Didn't Papa say the man was a miner? Could be while he was off digging for gold, his lady friend got tired of waiting?"

"Could be," Irene answered. She stared out at the garden. "I didn't just mean it was built with a woman in mind. It has a woman's touch. I can see a woman picking out the stained glass for the door, the mirror in the hallway, the fountain and flowers in the garden, the design for the kitchen. It's just hard to imagine a man with such a fine decorating sense. I mean everything just feels like a woman was involved."

"Maybe he planned on marrying someday and wanted it special for her, whoever she might turn out to be," Lillian said.

Sarah thought for a moment. "It's possible but I don't think so. Did you see that lovely mirror in the hallway?" She walked around, pulling her shawl closer about her. "There's a feeling about this house, can't you sense it?

"You're right. I can just see a woman walking from room to room, admiring the beauty of this place, the beauty that she created herself. Maybe the sister was responsible. Didn't they say he died before it was completed? Can't you feel it, Gram? Can't you just feel her presence?"

"What I feel is that this whole house needs a good airing. Let's open some windows, and start pulling some of these dust covers off. I'm dying to see what kind of furniture was left. I know you were surprised about the furniture, but if his sister married and had her own place, she probably chose her own furniture. If there were no other relatives, then there was no one to claim the furniture. You don't know how lucky we are. Can you imagine how much it would cost to furnish this place?"

Irene walked back into the dining room and began removing the white sheets from the table, chairs, and serving pieces. Lillian and Sarah followed her lead, and pulled cover after cover off the furniture.

Clayton and Joseph had already exposed the furniture in the parlor, library, and study, and opened the windows.

Irene and Sarah walked into the entryway at the same time the two younger children came clamoring down the stairs.

"We got our rooms picked out and Sarah chose the one she wants. There is a big room with a sitting room and dressing room attached. That'll be for Papa, and there are still four more vacant bedrooms left upstairs. This house is really, re-all-y b-i-i-g," Clay Jr. said, stretching his arms out from his sides. "It's big enough for everybody to live here."

"I noticed a large bedroom with a good size sitting room, and a water closet, just off the back of the study," Joseph said. "I think Irene and I should take that one. That way there would be someone downstairs to keep an eye on things, and a couple of extra pair of ears for any suspicious sounds. And I wouldn't have to climb those stairs every day."

"Papa Joe, what are you talking about?" Sarah cried, tears welling up in her eyes. "Do you mean that you and Gram might move out here with us? That would be too good to be true."

He smiled and glanced at Clayton, who nodded. "When your pa told me about this place, I figured if he felt that good about it, I could take a chance along with him, and stick my neck out. We went in together on the bid. Your papa didn't spend four hundred dollars. We put in two hundred each.

"We thought you all might get awfully lonely way out here, and I know your grandma would worry the dickens out of me to be driving out here all the time, checking up on y'all.

"Clay is right about hard times. Could be our place might be the next one sold right out from under us, plus, looks like y'all could use the help around here. It's time you had some help, Sarah.

"You have spent the past two years being an adult, while your pa worked. You need time to be a young girl. And there's a chicken coop to mend, barn and fences need repaired, and there's fields to plow, cows to milk and..."

"Oh, Papa Joe, I'm so glad." Sarah laughed and threw her arms around his neck.

"That is all right with you, isn't it, Bob?" Joseph asked, using his wife's pet name, peering at her over his granddaughter's shoulder.

Her birth name was Roberta Irene. He teasing-
ly called her Bob when he was feeling playful. She
knew when he called her Bob, he'd probably already
made up his mind, and just wanted her approval.

"I can't imagine living without my family."
Irene smiled and hugged her husband.

The children started whooping and dancing
around. Joseph beamed, while Sarah cried.

Clayton gave thanks that things seemed to be
working out for the best, considering it was such a
short time ago when he walked out of the mill office, and didn't know how long his family would have
a roof over their heads.

Everyone walked slowly around the house.
The furniture was beautifully hand-crafted and sturdy, polished to a fine sheen, and the upholstery was
lovely, soft, and durable. The women discovered two
sets of dinnerware. One, a soft cream-colored pot-
tery trimmed in blue, while the one in the display
cabinet was a service of delicate imported white
china, with tiny bouquets of roses sprinkled around
the edges.

In the buffet drawers they found a set of simple flatware, and a mahogany chest that contained
polished silver, with matching roses on each handle.
On the mantle, a small sailing ship decorated one
side of the fireplace, and on the other side, a large
bronzed eagle.

After a quick tour of the house, Joseph and
Clayton took Clay Jr. out to inspect the barn and
other out buildings.

Sarah and Lillian continued the linen check,
while Irene and Mary went to the kitchen to go
through the storage rooms, catalog supplies that

were still edible, and make a list of things they might need from town.

Irene sent Sarah to get a bucket of water from the well just outside the back door, while she went to the wagon to bring in the crate with the kettle and coffee pot. Irene noticed a coffee pot sitting on the stove, but wasn't sure when it had last been cleaned properly. She was ready for a cup of tea, and imagined that the others were too. She knew that Joseph and Clayton would soon be ready for coffee.

While the coffee perked and she waited for the kettle of water to come to a boil, Irene uncovered a fresh molasses cake she had baked the day before, and set the kitchen table for a snack.

Joseph and Clayton, with Clay Jr.'s grumbling help, continued to bring in boxes from the wagon, taking them to their respective rooms.

Sarah held the front door open for them and smiled sadly. "I wish Mama could see this," she said. She watched them bring in a box labeled *Mama's Things* and sighed sadly.

"I think she can," Clayton said softly. "I feel her smiling down on us right now, don't you?"

His daughter smiled. "I hope so, Papa. I truly hope so."

"I smell coffee. Let's go see what your Gram has for us."

With the coffee and tea poured, and slices of cake passed around, the little group talked about Eagle Creek.

"Does the inside of the house look like you thought it would?" Mary asked Lillian, between bites of cake.

"Actually, it's much more beautiful than I imagined," Lillian answered. "I've peeked through the windows, but with everything covered up, I couldn't see much. I've always loved this house. I guess every old house has stories behind them, and this one is no different. I grew up listening to my grandfather talk about Eagle Creek."

"Was your grandfather acquainted with the man who built this house?" Sarah asked.

"Oh, yes, they were close friends. Those were the days between the gold rush and the War Between the States, you know, before things got bad."

"Did your grandfather fight in the war?" Joseph's voice was low.

"He did enlist but with his banking experience, he was put in charge of procuring and managing the supplies for the units in this area. He was one of the few who never fired a shot."

"I'm sure your grandmother was relieved," Irene said softly, and looked lovingly at her husband.

Lillian took a sip of tea. "Grandma Martha used to say she was so blessed that Grandpa came home safe and sound. Mother was about ten years old then, and remembers when Grandpa rode home after Lee surrendered. You were just a child then, too, weren't you, Mister Martin?"

"Yes, I was almost eleven. I was lucky, too. My pa was shot but it wasn't serious. He never wanted to talk about it, though. There were very few people back then who didn't lose a family member in the war, fighting on one side or the other. The memory of what happened must have been horrible for those who went."

"No doubt it was."

"No more talk of war, please. That sad time is behind us now. With a new century, we have a time for new beginnings," Irene said."

"Here, here," Clayton agreed. "Let's toast to new beginnings."

He raised his coffee cup and the others imitated with their cups held high in the air, all murmuring their toasts.

With the coffee and tea cups empty and the cake eaten, the rest of the house was investigated thoroughly. Clayton agreed with Little Clay that he would take the large bedroom with the sitting area, and the attached dressing room. He told the children it was time to put the wagon in the barn and store the boxes in the proper rooms. Once downstairs, the children ran out to the wagon to see if they had forgotten anything.

Clayton started out the door, and Lillian joined him on the porch. "I'd be happy to finish helping y'all get settled in, Mister Wilkins but it's getting late, and Uncle William will be worried if I'm not home."

"You've done more than you should have, Miss Anderson. I have a feeling you're the kind of woman who likes to finish what you start, but we couldn't let you do that. You and your uncle have done enough for us.

"And I'm sure you're right, your uncle is probably peeking out the window this very minute, looking for your return. I know I would if one of my children was gone too long. Please tell him how much we appreciate his kindness. Thank you, too, very much, for all your time bringing us to our new home."

"It has been my pleasure, and I appreciate you allowing me to see the inside of this incredible house. I'm so glad to have met you and your beautiful family. You will all be such a wonderful addition to our lovely town. I hope I'll see you when you come into town."

"You're more than welcome, and please feel free to drop by and visit anytime. We're not much on formality here, so consider this an invitation for you to come by at your convenience, Miss Anderson."

"Please, call me Lillian. We're not much on formality either."

"I will, if you call me Clayton."

"I'd like that, Clayton. Don't bother the others, just tell them how much I enjoyed meeting them, and I'll see them again soon."

With a smile and a handshake, Lillian mounted her horse and waved. She galloped down the drive toward town.

After the unloading was finished, Irene and the girls started going through the boxes and putting things away. Joseph and Clay Jr. stored the wagon in the barn, and settled the horses down for the night. Joseph filled the water trough, and gave each horse a generous helping of grain, while little Clay explored the barn.

Clayton brought in firewood for the stove, and later in the evening Sarah fried smoked ham, and opened a couple of jars of potatoes and green beans, while Irene made a large pan of biscuits.

After they ate, Irene and Sarah cleaned up the kitchen, while Clayton and Joseph lugged in a couple of more armloads of wood for the next morning. Little Clay and Mary were sent to check to make sure all the lamps were filled with oil.

~ TWO ~
Unexpected Sounds

After enough wood had been piled in the kitchen wood box for breakfast the next morning, the family lit lamps and retired to the living room. A small fire crackled in the hearth, and Little Clay sat cross-legged on the floor, gazing heavy-lidded at the dancing flames.

"You know, this house just doesn't look like it's been vacant for very long. It almost looks like the occupants are just away for a short time. I keep waiting for someone to walk in the front door and inform us that we're in the wrong house," Sarah admitted nervously.

"It is most unusual that a magnificent house like this hasn't been claimed by a relative of the owner, or snatched up by someone rich who would divide it into smaller farms," Joseph said.

"Papa, why do you think we, of all people, were able to obtain all this for just four hundred dollars, an amount that wouldn't buy that gorgeous front door? It seems like a miracle, and I'm sorry but I just can't help thinking there's been a horrible mistake, and we're going to be left out in the cold once that mistake is corrected." Sarah frowned, looking around the room.

"When I bid on this house, one of my thoughts was that it would be a miracle if our bid was accepted. I'm not sure what we've done to deserve such a blessing, but I know that when I sign the papers to this house in the next few days, the deed will be handed over to us.

"Maybe it was your mother's unwavering love and faith in the good Lord that He would provide for us. Maybe it was our entire family pulling together, our strength never waning, ever struggling, depending on each other, and always being there for one another. Maybe we are just the recipients of a gift that was offered in love, and it's our duty to make sure that gift is accepted in love.

"Whatever it is, we have an obligation to make sure that gift lives on. Don't ask me how I know but that's the way it is. Will you all join hands and let's give a silent prayer of thanks to the Lord for this gift?" Clayton asked solemnly.

With heads bowed and hands clasped, each gave thanks for their new chance, though Sarah couldn't help but pray that there hadn't been a mistake.

"I'll have to confess I'm a little bushed," Papa Joe admitted. He arched his back and stretched his arms over his head. "If nobody minds, I think I'll hit the hay. Bob, you ready to turn in?"

"I am a little tired myself," Irene confessed. "I think bedtime is a good idea. Aren't you children tired, too? With all this excitement, you must be exhausted. I know I'm ready to stretch out on a soft bed with crisp clean sheets."

"Me, too," Little Clay squealed. "I get to sleep in my very own bed, in my very own, by-myself, all-alone room, without no girls to bother me."

"Without *any*, Clay Junior, without *any* girls," Sarah corrected. She had once dreamed of becoming a teacher and couldn't help teaching in her own way.

"That's what I said." Little Clay furrowed his brow, frowning at his sister.

"Never mind," Sarah sighed. "We'll talk about

your poor English tomorrow. It's time for everyone to get some rest. Tomorrow is just the beginning of many days of hard work. Hope we're all up to it. Let's go to bed."

~ * ~

Although Clay Jr. pretended to be thrilled about having his own room, he kept pacing up and down the hallway, peering wide-eyed into everyone's room until Sarah threatened to tell their father. It was he who first heard the strange howling shortly after everyone had blown out their lamps, and settled down to sleep.

Little Clay's eyes were heavy with fatigue and he felt himself slipping away. The first cry cut through the air like a tomahawk on the fly. The boy's eyes flew open. The hair on his arms bristled and he sat up in bed, listening and waiting. When it sounded again, he bolted from under the covers, raced down the hall into his father's room, and jumped into bed without slowing.

Clayton pulled on his overalls, took Little Clay in his arms, and after depositing him in bed with Mary, he started downstairs. Joseph met him by the back door, shotgun cocked and ready.

"Better check the barn door. If it's a hungry wolf, he might attack the horses," Papa Joe warned.

"Could be a coyote after those chickens," Clayton said, and held the lantern up before him. Cautiously, they walked toward the barn. "What did it sound like to you?" Clayton asked. "It didn't sound like any wolf or coyote I've ever heard. Could it have been an Indian?"

"I don't think so," Joseph said slowly. "They sound more like a wolf to us than a wolf does, and this didn't sound that wild."

"Who's out there?" Joseph yelled into the darkness. "We got guns, and don't think we won't use them. Get on your way and leave us alone. I don't want to shoot anybody, but I dang well will."

There was only silence. Not even the sound of insects or night birds could be heard. It was quiet... too quiet for comfort.

They walked around the barn, checked the horses, fastened the barn doors, and went back to the house.

Irene and the children were waiting in the kitchen, huddled by the back door.

"What was it, Pa? Did you see it? Did you scare it away?" Clay Jr. asked.

His hair bounced into his eyes when he jumped up and down, peering out the window.

"It was probably just a wild dog, Son. Didn't you say one of you heard a dog barking today? Nothing to worry about, I didn't find a thing. Whatever it was is gone now, and we need to get back to sleep.

"Papa Joe and I are going to hitch up the wagon and go back to Dawson Creek tomorrow. We'll need his wagon and ours to load up all their things. I think we can get everything into both wagons so we need get an early start."

"That's a good idea," Irene said. "We'll get everything put in its place, and settled in as soon as possible. Come on children, let's get to bed."

"Papa," Clay Jr. said. "Can I... can I..."

"Yes, Little Clay, you can sleep in my bed tonight. But it's time you get used to your own room, or talk one of the girls into sharing, 'cause it's just for this one night, you hear?" Clayton said firmly. He gently stroked the boy's hair and patted him on the back.

"Yes, sir," Clay Jr. said. He blushed and made little, invisible circles on the floor with his big toe.

~ * ~

By the end of the week, Joseph and Irene's belongings were delivered to Eagle Creek Farm. The girls helped their grandmother dust, sweep, and wash windows. Little Clay helped his father and Papa Joe repair the shutters, replace the hinges on the kitchen door, and start the long chore of checking fences for breaks in the rusty wire and rotten posts.

Lillian dropped by with a welcome basket filled with fresh ground coffee, cake, and even a couple of bags of candy for the children. Dressed for work, she volunteered to sweep the porch and wash the outside of the windows.

Irene couldn't help notice that Lillian had worn a split riding skirt and soft blue blouse, with a ribbon in her hair, instead of the rawhide tie. She also caught the young woman pinching her cheeks and smoothing her hair, before she rode off to take the noontime meal to the men.

As the cleaning progressed, Irene and Sarah continued the list of kitchen and cleaning supplies, while Joseph and Clayton noted all the feed, nails, and other essentials to make all the repairs needed. With the supply list growing longer, Clayton made plans for the trip to the town's general store, and he wanted to get the papers for the house signed so everything was legal.

~ * ~

After breakfast the following Monday, Clayton and Joseph saddled up the two plow horses, and harnessed the other two to one of the wagons. With Sarah at the reins and Irene beside her on the seat, Mary and Little Clay climbed into the back, each clutching a penny tightly in their fists for a visit to the store.

It took over half an hour to get to the little town, which was marked by a hand-carved sign reading, *Welcome to Sycamore Grove*. There were several small shops on either side of the street, with a wooden sidewalk running in front of each group of stores.

The largest building was the general store on the corner. A small tea shop, a hat shop specializing in the latest fashions, and a neat little dressmaker's cottage sat in a row past the mercantile. Farther on, there was a leather store with shoes and belts displayed in the window, and a blacksmith business at the end.

Across from the general store was the bank, and next to the bank was a land office. Next to that was the doctor's office, and the last business was the ticket office for the stage coach line. In the distance they could hear the whining and screaming saws of the busy sawmill.

Sarah pulled the wagon up to the rail in front of the general store, and they all climbed down. Joseph looked down the street and spotted the blacksmith, while the rest discussed where each wanted to go. Before they could decide which place to check out first, they heard a voice calling to them.

"Hello, there." Lillian Anderson hurried toward them, a wide smile on her pretty face. "I was hoping I'd be in town when you all came in."

Clayton jerked off his hat, so did Little Clay and Joseph.

"Oh please," Lillian said. "Don't do that. It makes things feel so formal. Didn't we get that straightened out earlier?" She smiled warmly, which caused her dimples to deepen.

Clayton couldn't help but return her smile. "It's good to see you. You make us feel at home."

"Well, you are home, and Sycamore Grove is a better place for y'all being here. Miss Irene, would you and the girls allow me to treat you to a cup of tea, and a delicious orange cake, at the Sugar 'N Spice tea shop? It will be a nice change to talk to you while sitting down instead of cleaning."

Irene smiled and nodded. "We'd be delighted."

"Thank you but I'd like to look around in the store," Mary said shyly.

"You can join us another time, Mary," Lillian said softly. "I know you are curious about the town."

"Joseph and I are going to look at a plow. You ladies can join us later," Clayton said. He turned and headed toward the store door.

"You go look at the plow, son," Joseph said. He stopped and peered down the street. "I want to check out the blacksmith down yonder. I'll be back directly."

Clayton nodded and led Mary and Little Clay inside.

The storekeeper looked up in surprise when he heard the bell, and watched the family file in.

"Good morning. Welcome to Barker's Emporium. I'm Robert Barker," said the small, bespectacled man. He approached them with his hand stuck out.

"Clayton Wilkins. Glad to meet you, Mister Barker." Clayton shook hands, and then pulled his list from his pocket.

"Passing through, are you? Where 'bouts y'all headin'?" Robert Barker asked, while rolling up his sleeves.

"Not passing through," Clayton explained. "We just bought a farm up in the hills. I'm Clayton Wilkins, and these are my two youngest, Little Clay and Mary. My oldest daughter, Sarah, is with my mother-in-law, and my father-in-law is at the blacksmith shop. We need a few supplies, thank you."

"Bought a farm, eh?" The little man mused. He rubbed his chin and stared at the floor, deep in thought. "Around here? Don't recall anyone moving away."

"It's down the road a ways, up in the foothills. It's called Eagle Creek," Clayton told him.

"Eagle Creek, you bought Eagle Creek? Well, ain't that something," Mr. Barker said, scratching his head.

He glanced toward the corner, where two men slowly rose, and came toward them. They were dressed in clothes that hadn't seen soap and water in several months, and obviously, the men hadn't bathed in quite some time from the odor emanating from them. Their hair was greasy and unkempt, and the crumbs and stains in their beards illustrated items of past meals.

One of the men stuck out his hand toward Clayton, who pretended not to notice.

"My name is Frank Owens, this is my brother Nate. We live down the road a bit on the other side of your place. We heard the old man that built that there house was crazy in the head. I thought his sister's youn'uns wuz a'livin' there. Are you a kin or sumpin'?"

"No," Clayton replied cautiously, inching back, away from the smell. "No, we're not. Here's my list, Mister Barker. Mary, you and Clay Junior look around a bit, and see if you find something to spend your penny on. I'll check out the tools and fencing supplies."

"Yes, sir," Robert said, taking the list, and glowering at the two loudmouth bullies.

Frowning, he jerked his head at the Owens' brothers, motioning them to go away, though they didn't seem to notice.

"Hope you folks ain't planning on hiring any farm hands from 'round here, 'cause iffen you are, you won't find 'em. Nobody'll work that place. It's hainted, you know," Frank Owens said, and followed Clayton. A guttural laugh bubbled from his lips, and he wiped his mouth on his stained sleeve.

"Been others, you know, wantin' ta buy that place," Nate chuckled and snorted. "He wouldn't have it, you know, the ghost of Mack Kaymey. He just wouldn't have it. He may be dead and gone but he ain't leavin' that place, no, siree, he ain't leavin'. You'll see. He'll run you off like he runned them others off, all but me 'n Nate. Now we'd con-sider working fer ya, that is, iffen the price wuz right."

"Frank, you and Nate collect your stuff and go on home now. Your pa'll be looking for you. You know he will," warned the store owner.

Nate's eyes twitched nervously. He glanced toward the door, while Frank snatched up their package.

"Mark my words, strangers ye be now and strangers ye'll always be. Ya won't last. They never do." He spat near Barker's foot, then turned and fol-lowed his brother out the door.

"What was that all about?" Clayton asked. He grimly watched the brothers swagger across the sidewalk toward their horses.

"Don't you pay them boys no mind, Mister Wilkins. Henry Owens Three is their daddy, and he's a good man but both his young'uns can't seem to grow up. Their ma was a wild one, she was, till she ran off and left them with their pa. They're like two thorns in his side. They were bullies when they were young boys, and they're lazy good-for-nothings now that they're older.

"There's another boy, little Henry Four, and he takes after his pa. Easy smile, friendly, and don't shy away from hard work. If you have any business there, he's the one to see.

"Old Henry keeps 'em in line most of the time, but they're like little Banty roosters, crowin' 'n flappin' their wings, trying to act tough when their pa's not around. Just don't pay 'em no mind, nobody around here does."

"No, I won't. I've met plenty of their type. But I meant what about the tale they were telling, the one about the place being haunted, and nobody wanting to work the place. I never intended on hiring hands but I'm curious," he said. "Tell me what you know about the original owner, I forgot his name."

"That'd be Mack. Mack Kaymey. Actually, I wasn't born when he moved here. My grandfather opened this store back then, and he knew him. So did my father. He helped out at the store back then.

"When I got older, there was an order my father needed delivered out there. I volunteered to take it, mostly out of curiosity, and that's one of the few times I ever saw that place close up, or Mister Kaymey's sister, too, for that matter. She was a lovely lady, sweet, kind, and always gave me an extra quarter for delivering.

"You can see, sir that I'm small in stature but Grampa used to say that Mister Kaymey was even smaller than me. Even with those tall boots he wore, he couldn't have been taller than five foot two or three, and Grampa said he bet he didn't weigh more than a hundred pounds.

"So he couldn't have been taller than five one or two when he was barefoot. He always wore a hat, coat, vest and gloves most of the time. He had several slaves and when he died, he left orders that they were freed, and even left them some land at the back of the property, but they stayed on and continued to work for his sister. Far as I know, they're still there. Come to think of it, his sister was tiny, too."

"What happened to Mister Kaymey?" Mary asked.

"Well, I remember hearing that he was sickly when he moved here. Story goes that he had a bad fall right here in town and struck his head. It didn't seem so bad at the time, but I guess with him being in ill health, it was too much for him. His sister came down to nurse him, and see to the building of the house he started, but he never recovered. He died shortly after his sister arrived and never got to see his house finished."

"That's so tragic," Clayton said sadly, "to die so young. Did he never tell anyone why he built such a huge house for just himself?"

"I don't think he ever told anyone anything. He was an extremely strange and solitary man. He'd come in, hand Grampa, or Pa, his list, and then wait in his carriage for the goods to be loaded. Sometimes his slaves would come with him and pick up the supplies.

"I guess the only folks he ever said more than two words to was his neighbor, Lucas Chase, and the banker, Ernest Gaines. Mister Gaines would never discuss Mack Kaymey with anyone. He said it was confidential and then he'd close his mouth, and that was that."

"What about those folks that worked for him?" Clayton asked.

"They keep to themselves. Come in once a month or so, picked up their supplies quickly, and then they're gone. There are a few other Negro families in the area, but they don't talk about themselves much."

"Now, tell me the reason no one will work or stay there," Clayton repeated. "Don't want my family in any danger if there's anything I can do to prevent it.

"I can't say for sure. It could be just an old mountain cat prowling round there, or a pack of wolves living up that way. It is a secluded area, Mister Wilkins, and hardly anyone passes by there. Folks say there's something there but you'd have to ask the people living on the back acres about that, and I seriously doubt they'll tell you anything.

"Most of those that looked at that house were city folks, and I imagine it looked pretty wild out there. I don't think they'd have ever been happy living there, or in town here, either. This just isn't the place they were looking for. They probably wanted to be a country gentleman but it was just too much country for them," he said with a chuckle.

Clayton smiled, too. He had met the same kind of city folks Robert was talking about and he, too, couldn't see most of them living at Eagle Creek

Farm. Maybe the store keeper was right. Maybe it was just too remote for those who had looked at it.

"Papa," a young man called from behind the counter.

"Sorry," Robert Barker said. "My son, Nathan, needs some help."

He rushed off to help his son at the counter, while another young man began boxing up his order. Clayton turned to see Joseph come in the store with a smile on his face.

"We're in luck, Clayton. I found a really good leather worker who can repair all our harnesses and saddles. He also works on wagons and buggies. He says there a fine buggy somewhere at the farm. The family who lived there had one, and he thinks it must still be there.

"I also checked with the blacksmith, and he makes house calls. He works on harnesses and halters, too. He's coming out next week to check the horses' shoes, and see if the plows need sharpening, or if he can fix anything else for us. He says the first trip is on the house. He's a really fine fellow.

"I think he just wants a look at the place. Apparently, the previous owners never let many people on the property."

Joseph grinned and waved at Irene, watching her, Lillian, and Sarah enter and go directly to the counter.

"Did you ladies have a good time?" He asked loudly. When they returned Joseph's smile and nodded, he turned toward Clayton.

"I've got a few things I need to pick up, too. I'll be ready to leave in just a minute," he told his son-in-law, then headed to join Irene at the counter.

"I'm going to the bank to sign the papers on

the house, and see about transferring our money here. It's always a good idea to get in good with the local banker. You never know when it might come in handy." Clayton grinned, walking toward the door.

"I may not impress him with our wealth," he chuckled, "but at least he'll know we're not penniless, and I must say, I am anxious to get a hold of that deed."

Clayton left the store, walked across the dusty street to the bank, and stepped into its cool interior. He started toward a teller, when the door to the back office opened. William Gaines walked into the lobby, looking at some papers he was holding.

"'Morning, William," Clayton said.

He felt uncomfortable calling the banker by his first name, even though Gaines had insisted he do so the day he picked up the house keys.

The banker looked up, smiled, and stuck out his hand. "Clayton, how are you? It's good to see you. Lillian is very impressed with your children, and Mister and Mrs. Martin. She went on and on about the house. Did your family come in with you today?"

"I couldn't get away without 'em. They were really anxious to see the town. Lillian took Sarah and Irene for tea, and to show them around."

"They are no more anxious to see the town than the town is to see them. We're not one of those stuffy little burgs that consider every newcomer an outsider. All of our ancestors came here from somewhere else. Every new citizen adds to our economy, and brings something into our social world. You are all welcome with open arms."

"I met a couple of yahoos in the general

store. I think they said their name was Owens. I don't think they were too glad to see us."

William snorted. "I don't imagine the town was very glad to see them around either. They aren't anything but trouble most of the time. Don't judge us by the Owens', please.

"Their father is a good man, and Henry Four is fair and friendly, but Nate and Frank must have been born sucking on a green persimmon. They've had a sour attitude since they could walk, and been an anvil around their father's neck from the time they were born.

"I imagine every town has its share of bullies and loudmouths—they're ours. If they give you any trouble, let me know. We don't hold with trouble-makers around here, and they know it."

Clayton shook his head. "Don't worry. Joseph and I can handle them. I think they're mostly hot air."

"You're right, of course. Now let's get down to the reason you're here."

He took Clayton's arm and headed toward his office. "Arnold, tell anyone who needs to see me I'll be busy for the next hour or so."

"I-I don't mean to take up much of your time," Clayton said. "I know you're a busy man, and I thought I'd just drop in and sign whatever it is I need to sign."

"Well, the signing is necessary but there's a lot about your new property that I need to tell you. That house has a story. It has been waiting for you and your family for about sixty years, and that tale will take some telling."

Clayton blinked hard at that strange remark, but allowed William to lead him into the office. The banker indicated a large, overstuffed chair and Clayton sat, while the banker proceeded around his desk to his chair.

William took out his keys, unlocked a drawer on the left side of his desk, and retrieved a thick, over-stuffed file, which he plopped on the top of his desk. A smile creased William's face. Suddenly, he jumped up and headed for a small table against the wall.

"Mister Wilkins, please forgive me. This calls for a celebration. Would you like a whiskey, or do you prefer cognac?"

"Neither one but I thank you kindly. I do see a pot of coffee there. Would coffee be too much trouble?"

"Coffee it is, Mister Wilkins. Would you care for cream and sugar?"

"One sugar, please."

William prepared two cups of coffee, handed one to Clayton, and carried the other to his side of the desk.

"Now to the business at hand," he said, rubbing his hands together. "I saw on your application that you lost your job when the cotton mill was bought out, what made you bid on Eagle Creek? Wasn't that a bit risky considering the circumstances?"

Clayton bowed his head, took a deep breath, and faced William Gaines. "I've faced circumstances a lot more devastating than just losing a job. I lost my wife to pneumonia a few years ago, and my children lost their mother and best friend. She was my light and reason for living.

"My daughter reminded me that Susan, my wife, always thought the Lord posted opportunities for his children on a heavenly bulletin board, and when I saw the notice of this auction on the bank's bulletin board, I took it for a sign—a sign that this was my opportunity.

"I want a future for my children, and I want to give a secure home to Joseph and Irene, Susan's parents. To make a long story shorter, I followed my heart, I made the bid, and here I am. Sounds foolish when I say it out loud," Clayton said with a harsh laugh. "But that's the truth of it."

"My dear, young friend, it doesn't sound foolish at all." William pulled out his handkerchief, wiped his eyes, and blew his nose. "I think that is the most touching, inspiring reason I've ever heard. I admire and respect a man who dedicates his life to the people he loves."

"William, if you don't mind, could you tell me a little about the history of the house, and why all the secrecy of the bid, and the information y'all required?"

"That's what this meeting is all about, I assure you. You and I have a long friendship ahead of us, I can tell."

"That sounds mighty good."

"Well, Clayton, Eagle Creek was named after the stream that originates up in the hills where the eagles roost. The Indians were the first to call the land and stream Eagle Creek, and as it fits so well, the name stuck. The land of Eagle Creek went unimproved for many years until Ralph Duncan, the self-appointed mayor of Sycamore Grove, heard rumors that a cotton gin and mill was coming to town.

"Ralph was a widower, and his children were all grown and moved up north. He bought up the nearly thousand acres of land, built a small cabin, and waited for all the people he thought would be flocking here for jobs. He expected to sell the land off in small sections. He planned on keeping some of the woodlands to open a lumber mill for all the cabins he anticipated would be built on the sections he sold.

"Well, you already know the gin went in over at Dawson City. There weren't any people flocking to Sycamore Grove, and since Duncan had invested all his money in the property, he was heart-broken and became depressed. He lived out there like a hermit for a few years, and finally passed away.

"None of Ralph's children lived close by, or were interested in the property, and didn't want to bother paying taxes on such folly. They were embarrassed enough that their father had been so foolish, and lost all the money they thought would be their inheritance on an unsuccessful venture. Not only did they turn their back on the property, they didn't even have the good graces to attend his funeral."

William shuffled the papers until he found the one he wanted. "Here is the original transfer deed that starts the story of your purchase.

"My father was an instrumental part of this saga and when he retired, I discovered his daily journal, which he used diligently throughout his life. In it, he details the creation of Eagle Creek Farm, and the building of the manor. Seems to me, the part that's of interest to us, talks about the day he met the soon-to-be owner of Eagle Creek.

"A young man, who introduced himself as Mack Kaymey, came to see my grandfather in mid-fall 1857. The way Grandfather told it, the young man reported that he and his father had struck gold in California, and were traveling east when his father became ill and succumbed to the fever. The young man had no place to call home and was looking for a place to put down roots, and thought Sycamore Grove might be that place.

"Grandfather took him out to the piece of property, which was then called Duncan's Folly by the locals, and showed him the nearly one thousand acres, and the cabin. Apparently the young man was really impressed with the place, and agreed to buy it then and there."

William paused and took a long swig of coffee. Clayton was mesmerized by the story, and almost forgot he was holding a full cup, too. He took a drink and then waited silently for William to continue.

"It was that day, Grandfather used to say, that the straight path of his life made a sudden left turn. The young man reluctantly confessed that he wasn't a man after all, but a young woman named Aimee Amelia McKay, who had survived the sinking of the S.S. Central America. She was escaping an abusive relationship, and unfortunately, her means of escape led her to the ship caught in that vicious hurricane.

"A day, or so, after the hurricane roared itself out, that very ship eventually sank off the coast of Charleston from storm damage. Grandfather had, of course, heard of the tragedy since the ship had been carrying over a million dollars of gold from the gold fields of California. The banks and savings and loans companies suffered greatly from the loss of the expected gold.

"They had loaned out hundreds of thousands of dollars, and were depending on that shipment to reinforce those loans. It was a financial disaster for many banks, and it affected the East Coast economy severely.

"She swore my grandfather to secrecy concerning her identity, and Miss McKay only told him because she wanted the property to be legally hers, and knew it would be against the law if she were to buy it under a false name.

"To shorten this part of the story, I'll just tell you that my grandfather and Aimee McKay became the closest of friends. Since Grandfather was also a lawyer, he was able to get her name legally changed, and made sure the property became hers. With a new name, the property was hers, and that man she was running from couldn't track her by her last name.

"She called her place Eagle Creek Farm, later, after the house was built, it came to be known as Eagle Creek Manor. She told Grandfather that the gold indeed came from the gold fields, though not gathered by her hand. She had befriended an old man while on board the S.S. Central America who, when the ship was sinking, forced her to take his money belt and carpet bag filled with gold, since he could not swim, and knew he would not survive. He wanted his gold to benefit Aimee for her kindness, and knew that he could depend on her to make sure the gold was put to good use."

William rose and walked slowly across the room. He grunted as he struggled to open the window. Taking a deep breath of fresh air, he smiled at Clayton, and refilled their coffee cups.

"I'll shorten it again, and perhaps later you can find someone to fill in the details. Some escaped slaves hid in the woods on the back of the farm. One of the families was named Washington, and they also became close friends with Miss McKay. She offered them a proposition and, again, Grandfather stepped in and created false ownership papers showing the slaves belonged to her. She never intended owning them, the papers were just for their protection.

"A man named Lucas Chase bought the property next to hers, and although it's hard to believe, he, too, had been a survivor of that same ship. In time, he learned Miss McKay's true identity and they became close, very close indeed.

"This was a dramatic turn of events since her past began to catch up with her. She discovered the man who abused her, and forced her to run away, still searched for her. Her friends banded together and the man was arrested and jailed for the many crimes he had committed." William chuckled and shook his head.

"Miss McKay's small band of conspirators was my grandfather, the town doctor, Lucas Chase, his houseman, Rose Washington, and a Marshal—I forget his name. My grandfather, the doctor, and Mister Chase conjured up a sister for Mack Kaymey, and they proposed he would become ill. Miss McKay became that sister, and appeared to arrive to care for him, but unfortunately, he wouldn't survive.

"Now, Aimee McKay became Amelia Kaymey. They did this because Aimee didn't want the town folks to feel that she had used them, duped, or tricked them. She wanted to live among them without any hard feelings.

"She and Lucas married, and they lived in the Chase house, but went back and forth between there and the house she built. When their daughter, Rosalie, was born, she lived at Eagle Creek until she grew up, married, and she and her husband moved up north.

"Aimee and Lucas took care of the place until they passed away a few years ago. Then, as stated in Aimee's will, if the children decided to live elsewhere, the house would be put under the care of the bank, and we would find appropriate owners."

William paused when he noticed a concerned frown on Clayton's face. "Don't concern yourself about Rosalie. Amy left her a great deal of money. Enough, in fact, for her to build several houses like Eagle Creek Manor."

"That's good to know but what do you mean by *appropriate owners*?"

"Mrs. Aimee McKay-Chase had very specific notions as to the type of people to own her house. They had to be kind, loving, hardworking, down on their luck, and willing to take a chance. She wanted the house in the hands of someone who would appreciate the love and sacrifice the house was built on. She wanted them to be the kind of people who would reach out to others, and spread the happiness this house could bring. Your application and bid fit her list perfectly, so, like you said earlier—here you are."

William took a deep breath and watched Clayton carefully. "It was important to Aimee that the house be lovingly cared for and, one day, when no one in your family cares to live there, it will be passed on to another family with the same attributes."

"We're supposed to give up our house?" Clayton asked with a look of disbelief.

"Oh no, you misunderstand me. The house belongs to you all right, and your children, and their children, and on and on, as long as there is any relative to pass it on to. But if the day comes when, or if, there is no family left, then she would like you to leave a stipulation in your will that the house be passed on to someone like yourselves. Does that sound reasonable?"

"Mister Ga—excuse me—William," Clayton said. "My family and I consider this house and land a blessing, and blessings should be appreciated and, if possible, shared with others. I would be honored to make sure this fine lady's house is enjoyed by my family, and when there is no one left around here to take possession of it, I will make sure the house passes on to a deserving family. I give you my word, and will sign a paper guaranteeing it."

"That's all I wanted to hear. The committee that chose you, and your family, to have the house, are descendants of Aimee McKay's closest friends. After reading your application, and doing a little investigating, there is no doubt that you and your family are definitely the kind of people Aimee wanted to have in the house.

"Let's get those papers signed. I know you have a lot of settling in to do, and are working hard to get all the repairs done. There shouldn't be a lot to do. The bank did monthly checks on the property and kept it up as much as possible. By the way, I guess you were told the taxes are paid up for a while? You won't have to worry about that for the next five years."

"That does take a load off my mind. We have enough left after paying the bid for some improvements and supplies, until our crops come in next year. I am surprised there was so much nice furniture left. Didn't Miss McKay's daughter want it?"

"Rosalie did take a few pieces that were special to her mother, but wanted the new owners to enjoy the rest. She knew that was what her mother wanted."

"Well, my family is thrilled. I could never have given them things like that."

"My dear friend, you just did. It was your life-style, changing your life around, and the devotion to your family, and your wife's family, that provided the house, land, and all that comes with it. Don't sell yourself short. It was all you."

"Thank you, sir," Clayton replied, tears stinging his eyes. "You don't know how I appreciate those words."

"I only speak the truth, Clayton. Now let's get those papers signed so you can get your business done, and get on your way to your new home.

"Oh, I must ask a favor of you. I would appreciate it if you would keep this story to yourself for a while, and when you share it with your family, ask them not to discuss it too freely. There are still a few old-timers around that remember Mack Kaymey, and I don't think Miss Aimee would want them to know the truth about her identity. She always worried about their feelings."

"That's an easy favor to grant. I'm not sure I'd tell it right anyway. Miss Aimee's secret is still safe, I assure you."

When Clayton finished at the bank, he found everyone in the wagon ready to go home, while Lillian stood by talking to Irene. Although they seemed relaxed, he could see worry in Sarah's eyes. He untethered the horses, and went to his daughter, who was holding the reins. He stepped up on the wheel and gently touched her shoulders.

"Well?" she asked nervously. "Was there any trouble? You can tell me, Papa. Was there a mistake?"

"Relax, honey. The house is ours free and clear." He waved the envelope William gave him. "This is our deed. That bulletin board in Dawson City was indeed the one the good Lord intended for us to see. The furniture and everything on the property belongs to us now—us and your grandparents. We don't have to pay taxes for quite a while, so we have enough to live on. I want you to step out of your mother's shoes now and enjoy life."

Sarah Wilkins' smiled, and then laughter bubbled up. She reached for Clayton, he hugged her tightly, and kissed her forehead tenderly.

"Did you get everything you needed?" he asked, stepping down.

"We got everything. Let's go home," Sarah said.

"Lillian, that invitation still stands. You come by and visit us now. I'm sure the ladies will appreciate your company." Clayton hesitated, examining his boots. "I guess we'll all appreciate your company," he added before swinging into the saddle.

"Thank you, Clayton. I will." Lillian smiled and her eyes seemed to twinkle.

It pleased him they were all laughing and talking. The pressure, tension, and worry were gone. It was time to live.

"We've got a couple of stops to make before we head home. William gave me the names of a couple of folks that will sell us a cow or two, and a few chickens. Maybe the new chickens will coax those wild ones into the pen."

"Oh, boy, we'll have eggs and milk. Can we get some hogs, Papa? And maybe some ducks and rabbits and..." Little Clay bounced up and down.

"Whoa, son, let's not get ahead of ourselves. We can't afford anything that doesn't contribute back to the family. Cows give milk, chickens give eggs but somehow I can't see you getting excited if we try to eat a duck or rabbit that you've raised as a pet. Maybe that can come later when our first crop comes in but for now, it's got to be the bare essentials. Understand?"

"Yes, Papa," the boy answered quietly.

"Joseph, we may need to go back and pick up a few bags of chicken feed. Could be the man with the cow can sell us a few loads of hay."

Clayton turned his horse, and Sarah pulled on the reins. The horses made a full circle, and they headed back to Barker's Emporium.

~ * ~

With a cow tied to the back of the wagon, and Mary holding a crate of laying hens, with two sacks of chicken scratch in back, and Little Clay holding a crate containing two squawking ducks, the family pulled into the side yard of their new home.

Sarah grinned and Mary kept nudging her, as they watched Little Clay struggle to get down from the wagon with two flapping, quacking, feather-flying ducks fighting to escape the crate.

Clayton untied the cow and led her to the barn, while Joseph rushed to the chicken pen to open the gate. Once inside, the girls opened the wooden cages and freed the chickens. Little Clay was right behind Mary, and when she moved aside, he shoved the struggling ducks through the opening, into the pen with the chickens.

He spit feathers and brushed duck droppings off his pants, and glanced at his sisters, who were fighting the urge to laugh. He grinned sheepishly, walked to the pen, and peered through the wire at his ducks. They were preening and pecking at their ruffled feathers.

"Well, son, you got your ducks. Your grandpa said they were his gift to you for your next birthday. They're your responsibility now. You can clean out that pond over there 'cause they'll be wantin' to get into water as soon as they can. You'll have to help the girls feed them and the chickens, make sure they have fresh water, keep the pond free of debris, and attach the crates on the wall of the coop and put fresh hay in them, for the hens to lay their eggs."

"All for a couple of unfriendly ducks," Little Clay said, shaking his head.

"All for a couple of frightened ducks," Irene corrected. "Every decision has an action, and for every action, there's a consequence. You must take responsibility for your decisions and actions, and learn to face the consequences. Life can be compli-cated, Clay Junior, and now is the perfect time to start learning that."

"Yes, ma'am," he said, digging the toe of his shoe in the dirt, his habit when embarrassed.

Bobbie Shafer

~ Three ~
New Neighbors, New Friends

"Children, go change into your work clothes, fold up your good clothes, and put them away. When you get the feed put up, come back and help unload the supplies." Irene grabbed a box and started into the house.

Once the supplies were in the house, Mary went into the chicken pen and started naming the hens. Joseph and Clayton stored away the farm supplies, while Sarah and Irene prepared supper.

Little Clay stood in the yard wondering what he should do, when a sound caught his attention. He listened carefully, trying to block out the chicken noises, and the voices of his father and grandfather. He couldn't be sure but he thought he heard it again.

He walked slowly across the backyard, his head cocked to one side, and pushed his way through the weeds at the edge of the clearing. He peered into the small grove of trees a little ways past the fence. He saw a movement, then another, and he took off at a steady trot.

"Here, boy, come here."

He whistled the best he could, and continued looking and listening. It was a dog. He remembered Mary heard one the first day they arrived. He might be hungry—he might need a home—he might need Clay Jr.

"Here doggie, come on, I won't hurt you."

He clapped his hands and tried to whistle again. The bushes moved again and a boy stood up. Little Clay froze in his tracks.

"Hey," the boy said, ducking his head, peering up through dark lashes.

He wore knee-length cutoffs, a sleeveless shirt, and no shoes. He stood and grinned at Little Clay, his dark eyes twinkling. A big, black and white dog, wagging his tail furiously, sat by his side.

"Hey," Clay responded.

"Y'all just move in?"

"Yeah, last week," Little Clay said. He watched the boy and cautiously moved closer. "You live 'round here?"

"Uh-huh," the boy nodded. "My name's Albert. What's yours?"

"I'm Clayton, well, Clayton Junior. My papa is Clayton, too," he said in a low voice.

"Well, I was named after my grampa. They call him Big Albert."

"At least you're called by your name. Most of the time they call me Junior, or Little Clay. Where'd you say you live?"

The boy turned half-way around, and jerked his head over his shoulder. "Oh, back there a bit. Grampa and Pa used to work here till... well... till Master Kaymey died. Then they worked for his sister. They don't work fer nobody now." He scratched his head and asked, "You like to fish?"

Little Clay nodded. "You bet I do. Where do you fish around here?"

"There's a big pond on the other side of the woods, a wide creek over there a bit, and a river 'bout three miles from here. They's lots of places to fish. Maybe we can go sometimes... you know... together," he said and hesitated, dropping his head. "That is, iffen your folks'll let you go with me."

"Sure they will. Why don't you come and meet my Pa? He and my grandpa, Papa Joe, are in the barn."

"Naw, I don't think so. They might not like you talking to me."

Clay Jr. frowned. "That's dumb. Why wouldn't they?"

"'Cause you're white and well, I'm not. Look, I'll be back tomorrow. You ask 'em, 'n iffen they don't care, and iffen you can, bring a pole, or we can cut one. I'll bring everything else, okay? Bye."

Before Clay could respond, Albert turned and disappeared into the woods.

"Papa," Clay called, running toward the barn, "Papa?"

"Here, son, what's the matter?"

"I just met a boy in the woods. His name is Albert. His pa and grandpa used to work here a long time ago. His grandpa is named Albert, too. They live back there somewhere. He wants to know if I can go fishing with him. Can I, Pa, can I? He's afraid you won't let me," Clay Jr. gushed.

"What do you mean he's afraid I won't let you? Why wouldn't I?"

Little Clay's brows knit together, and he thought for a moment. "I don't rightly know, Pa. He said you might not like me talking to him 'cause I'm white and he's not. What does that mean?"

Clayton smiled and looked back at Joseph, who smiled and shook his head.

"Little Clay, you can play with Albert all you want to, and I think it's really nice of him to ask you to go fishing. You tell him that for me. Tell him that he and his family are welcome here anytime. We would be proud to meet our neighbors."

"Pa, why did he think you wouldn't like him?" The boy looked anxiously at his father, his eyes wide with innocence.

"Son, you're only eight-years-old and haven't been soiled by the stupidity of mankind. Some people don't like other people, not because they don't agree with their politics, not because they don't agree with their religion, not because of any good reason except they don't like the color of their skin.

"They don't take the time to get to know people before they judge them. Chinamen came over, built our country a rail line, and got treated worse than a mangy dog. Colored folks were kidnapped and shipped over in chains to work the fields and make the plantation owners rich, and were treated worse than the Chinamen.

"I'm sure Albert didn't judge us. He was just afraid we would judge him. You understand, son?"

"I'm not sure. I kinda see what you mean but it sure sounds stupid to me."

"I agree, my boy, I agree. When Papa Joe and I get finished here, I'll help you find a good, straight sapling for a fishing pole. Think I got some cord and a hook or two in one of the boxes in the shed. I'll look after a while. You run on in and tell your Gram and sisters about your new friend, and our neighbors."

~ * ~

The next morning, Little Clay rose early, hastily threw the covers over his bed, yanked on his clothes, gobbled down his breakfast, and flew out the back door to prepare for his fishing trip with Albert. He said a quick, silent prayer that his new friend wouldn't be too frightened to return.

The men had scoured the nearby woods and found a straight, strong, young sapling for a pole. Clayton located his box of fishing hooks and a ball of twine, while Joseph dug in the rich forest dirt and filled a jar with dirt and a couple of dozen large earthworms.

Every so often, Clay Jr. ran to the spot where he had met Albert and called his name. He was so anxious to spend time with his new friend, the day seemed to drag on slowly. Little Clay just about gave up on his friend coming back. However, after lunch, Albert finally showed up—and he wasn't alone. When he walked out of the woods, Clay Jr. saw the large, broad shouldered man, and a boy a couple of years older than Albert with him.

"Hey," Albert said, and waved.

"Hey," Little Clay said, and backed up a few steps.

He was slightly intimidated by the tall man and muscular young boy, but his face couldn't contain the joy at seeing his friend. A wide, happy grin spread across his face.

"This is my pa, and this is Amos, my brother. They jest wanted to make sure your pa didn't mind you going with me," he said.

"Hi," Clay Jr. said and nodded. "My pa's just over there. He said I was supposed to tell Albert thank you for inviting me, and that y'all are welcome at our house anytime. Would you like to meet him?"

The man nodded but Albert's brother looked grim and unhappy at the prospect.

Little Clay turned and motioned for them to follow, and started for the barn, calling for his father.

"Pa, they're here. Albert brought his dad and his brother."

When Clayton heard his son, he walked to the

barn door and saw the group heading toward them.

"Joe, I guess Albert's family decided to check us out. Can't say that I blame them, with things the way they are."

"Pa, this is Albert, his pa and his brother," Clay Jr. said, motioning to his new friend.

"Welcome to Eagle Creek Farm. I'm Clayton Wilkins, and this is my father-in-law, Joseph Martin. When my son told us he had met a friend around his own age who wanted to go fishing, we were very glad. He has two sisters but I'm afraid they're not interested in playing with him." He stuck his hand out to Albert's father.

The man hesitated for a moment, and then responded by grabbing Clayton's outstretched hand and pumping it vigorously.

"Thank you, sir. My name is Isaac Washington, and this is my son, Amos. When Albert told us new folks had moved in, and there was a boy who wanted to go fishing with him, I had to see for myself. People aren't always what they seem, especially to young boys. I hope you don't take this visit as a threat."

Clayton smiled. "Never crossed my mind. You did what every good father would do—make sure their son wasn't in any danger. Please, Mister Washington, won't you and Amos join us for a cup of coffee? You can meet the rest of my family and tell us about yourself. After all, we are neighbors, and we may need each other's help from time to time."

"Are you sure your Mrs. won't mind?" Isaac asked.

Clay shook his head. "Little Clay told us all about meeting Albert yesterday, and we've been anxious to meet him and his family. Please, if you have a few minutes to spare."

Isaac looked at Amos, who had relaxed some-what, and shrugged. "Well, I guess we have little time."

"Son, run tell your Gram that we have com-pany, and to put on a fresh pot of coffee."

Clay Jr. pulled Albert's sleeve, jerked his head toward the house, and the pair took off.

By the time Clayton and the others reached the house, Sarah and Irene were in the kitchen, pre-paring coffee, and placing slices of cake on plates, while Mary set the table with cups and saucers.

"Irene, girls, this is Albert's father, Isaac Washington, and his brother, Amos. These are our neighbors who own property in the back corner. They came by to make sure Albert was in good hands. Isaac, these are my daughters, Sarah and Mary, and this is their grandmother, Irene."

Irene stepped forward and offered her hand. "Mister Washington, I am very happy to meet you. Little Clay is so excited to have met a new friend. I'm looking forward to meeting the rest of your fami-ly."

Isaac's eyes narrowed for just an instant be-fore taking her hand.

"I was afraid Al had misread y'alls welcome. I'm glad I was wrong," Isaac said, and shook Irene's hand.

After everyone sat at the table, Irene poured coffee, and the girls passed out cake.

"Do you have other children, Mister Washing-ton?" Irene asked.

"The name's just Isaac, ma'am. Yes, I have quite a few. There's..."

He scratched his head and looked puzzled. He

glanced at Amos, who laughed.

After wiping his mouth, Amos said, "They's seven of us, ma'am, plus Ma, Pa, Grandpa, and Uncle Rufus. Pa forgets how many we are, and forgets our names now and then. My sister, May, is expecting the first grandchild. Pa'll probably just call her Baby."

They all started laughing and Joseph burst into a coughing fit. "I'd forget, too. I have trouble keeping the two girls straight. That's quite a handful."

"How does your wife manage?" Irene asked. "I can't imagine handling that many. I have my hands full with these three."

"She's a blessing, that one, I must admit," Isaac said. "Her name is Ruth, and she never hears no bad news. Every problem is a challenge that she feels is her destiny to meet and conquer. I can't take no credit for the way my youn'uns turned out. It was all her, every step. They is all good, hard-working, dependable, Bible-readin' children, and each one is a star in my crown. 'Scuse me fer braggin'."

Irene smiled. "Please don't apologize. It's wonderful to hear a man speak so highly of his wife and children. I'm sure they are a great help to you and their mother. And it doesn't hurt to have children to help work your place. How many acres do you have, Mister, um... Isaac?"

"Master Kaymey deeded us each forty acres of good land. We make a fine living off it. There's plenty of cleared land to plow for vegetables, and there's lots of fruit and nut trees everywhere. Me and the youn'uns plants the crops, and the whole family helps with the harvest.

"The women folk cans what we needs, and we takes the rest to sell. My wife and her mother puts up some of the finest peach, plum, and fig jam and jellies you ever ate. I'll have her bring you some real soon."

"Is your mother there, too?" Irene asked.

"No, ma'am, she's gone now. It's just my Pa and my Cousin Rufus, and a few other families. Rufus is a blacksmith and a fine one, too. He keeps all our equipment in good working order. He'd be happy to work on yours. His grandpa did that same work when Master Kaymey was still alive."

"I notice you call the previous owner *master*. Were you his slaves? I understand you were freed when he died," Joseph asked, and took a sip of coffee.

"Now that's another story," Isaac murmured, his eyes darting across the table.

"Mister Washington, I realize we've just met, but you must understand, and trust us when we tell you that we don't believe in slavery, never did. What went on between you and Mister Kaymey is none of our business, and we apologize if we made you uncomfortable," Clayton said.

Again, Isaac gave Amos a look before he continued. "Mister Wilkins, my family wuz runaway slaves hiding on this land when Master Kaymey bought it. He found out when I got curious and snuck down to see who was living here. Mister Kaymey didn't approve of slavery either, and he agreed to pretend we belonged to him. He even had papers drawn up to prove his ownership of the family, so we would be safe from them that wuz hired to find people like us.

"We escaped from a wagonload of slaves

headin' west. A few bounty hunters came lookin', of course, but Master Kaymey soon sent them on their way. She... I mean *he* gave us not only our freedom but our lives... and our futures. There was my grandma, ma and pa, pa's brother, and some others that got away. The bounty hunters captured a couple.

"My family worked for Master Kaymey, and he was as good to them as if they were his own family. He gave them that land about five years after building the house. He gave 'em the land and our papers of freedom. He left them a little money, too, but no one knew, of course, except the Master and Mister Gaines, the lawyer. We all found out after he died.

"The marshal asked my grandpa what they were going to do since Mister Kaymey had passed, and when they showed him the deed and freedom papers, he was satisfied. He was a good man, he wuz. He told my pa he was to call him if there wuz any problems.

"That's about all there is to say about us. We're simple folks. We works the land, raise our youn'uns, takes care of the old ones, and reads the Bible. I'm satisfied with our life. Well, that's enough 'bout us. What brings you folks here?"

"I lost my job when a company up North bought out the company I worked for in Dawson City. I saw this house posted at the bank for auction, put in a bid, and here we are. No money to speak of, but strong backs, and even stronger determination to make a new life. Living here will be a good life for us and the children." Clayton paused and took a deep swig of coffee. "We'll try to be good neighbors, Isaac. We hope you'll call on us if you need to. We all need a friend, and we all need help now and then."

"That's very kind of you Mister Wilkins. Those are the exact words Mister Kaymey used when he met me and my folks all them years ago. I'll tell my family that we have good people livin' here, and they can relax." He rose and shook Clayton's hand. "It's been a real pleasure meetin' y'all."

"Isaac, you said your family received the land after the house was built, but I understood that the owner died before the house was complete."

"Y-yes, yes he did. I meant that Mister Kaymey's will gave the land to our family, along with the freedom papers. It was a while ago and I was young. I disremembered the details. I just got confused."

"That's understandable. I can hardly remember anything that happened when I was ten, except the fish I caught, the caves I explored, and some of the naughty things I did." Clayton grinned.

"I leave all the fact 'memberin' to my wife. She's good at that," Isaac said.

"Mister Washington, please tell your wife, I'm looking forward to meeting her and her mother. Tell them we're usually home, and they are welcome to drop by anytime," Irene said.

"I'll tell her, ma'am. She and her ma were really scared about Albert comin' here. They will probably be by to meet ya in a few days. My ma and pa worked for Mister Kaymey, and they were really close friends. It's nice to be able to see this house filled with good people once more.

"When my wife was a young girl, she sold berries and melons to Mister Kaymey's sister. Thank you for inviting her. I know she'll be anxious to drop by."

"No thanks needed. I will enjoy the visit,"

Irene assured him.

"Come on, now, Amos, we best get on home. Your ma'll think we done got ourselves in trouble. Nice to have met y'all," he said, nodding to Amos as he stood.

"Albert, you be home before dark, ya hear?" Isaac said firmly.

"I will, Pa, I will. Come on, Little Clay. Let's git our poles."

Clayton rested his arm around the young dark skinned boy's shoulders. "Son, I need to know where you boys are planning to fish. I'm not too familiar with the farm yet, and I'll need to be able to find you if there's an emergency."

Isaac told Clayton how to get to the pond and both boys said they would be back before dark. They took off laughing, swinging their bucket of worms, gripping their poles.

Irene walked into the backyard and watched the boys disappear into the woods.

"Hello, Mrs., are we intruding?" A hesitant voice came from the corner of the house.

Irene turned and smiled at the two women standing before her. She could tell by the familiar smile that one was young Albert's mother. The resemblance was remarkable.

"I have to confess that me and Rosa here followed Isaac and Amos when they brought Albert to meet yer boy. I wuz a little worried and had to see for myself that he waren't in no danger. We stayed in the woods till they started home, and when they told us how nice y'all were, and that it wuz okay to meet you, we reckoned now wuz as good a time as any. We ain't botherin' you is we?"

"Not at all, please come in. I'm Irene Martin,

and I was just about to put on a fresh pot of coffee."

"My name is Ruth, and this is my daughter Rosa." The small, dark skinned woman nodded toward the young girl standing behind her.

"Please come in. I have two granddaughters who will be happy to see someone their own age."

Irene held the back door open for the women, and called for Sarah and Mary. When the sisters arrived, introductions were made, and all the women sat around the kitchen table.

"I've always loved this old house," Ruth said with a smile. "I used to pick berries, nuts, and wild plums, and Miss Amelia would buy nearly all I could bring. She always invited me in and offered hot chocolate in the winter, and iced lemonade in the summer. My husband, and his pa and ma, worked for her for many years."

"Did you know the man who built the house?" Sarah asked.

Ruth looked down and took a sip of coffee. "No, I never met Mister Kaymey. He was gone before we moved here. Isaac's ma worked for Mister Kaymey until he died, and then for his sister for a long time. She loved that woman, she did."

"Was it Mister Kaymey or his sister that put in the garden back there?" Irene asked.

"Well, as I reckon it, Mister Kaymey designed the garden, but it was Miss Amelia that put all them plants in. She loved that garden, she did. When I'd bring berries by, she'd be out there kneelin' and weedin', and I couldn't hep but join her.

"Even after all this time, it pained me so to see it go to seed. I guess you kin tell that I drops by now and then and digs some to keep it lookin' fairly good. I guess it hepped me think of them still bein' here."

"Keeping something they loved alive does that, doesn't it? It just didn't look as neglected as the rest of the yard."

"Miss Amelia kept most of the men in the camp employed in one way or another, and they's the ones who kept the front garden up, and all the grasses cut down, and them vines from jest takin' over. It's a job me and Rosa just couldn't git done."

"Of course not. You did enough keeping the back garden looking so nice. The girls and I will take it over now, and rest assured, we'll keep the memory of your dear friends alive."

"That's mighty fine of you. I know Mister Kaymey and Miss Amelia wanted that garden to bring you as much joy as it did them."

Light conversation followed. The girls chattered away about chores and little brothers, while Irene and Ruth talked about housekeeping, sewing, and cooking. The visit was short but fruitful. Friendships formed and each was comfortable with the children playing back and forth.

When Ruth and Rose left, Ruth promised to return, and to bring her mother along for the next visit. Irene was anxious to meet the woman who knew so much about the man who built the house.

~ FOUR ~
An Offer You Can't Resist

Early one beautiful fall morning, a stranger strolled up the road. Joseph was at the stone wheel sharpening an axe when he heard the man whistling. He called for Clayton, and they both watched waited for him to approach.

The visitor was a tall, handsome young man with an easy smile and laughing eyes. Dressed in worn but clean work clothes, with a bundle slung over one shoulder, he walked with one hand stuffed in his pocket.

He pulled his hand out and touched his hat in greeting. "Afternoon, folks, beautiful day, isn't it?"

Clayton nodded and wiped his hand on a rag from his hip pocket.

"Sir, my name is Daniel Jones and this is your lucky day. You're probably thinking that this young whippersnapper's still wet behind the ears, and I don't have time to listen to his rooster crowing, but you'd be wrong, yes siree, you'd be wrong.

"I've worked since I was a small lad, and have been learning at the knees of some of the most talented men I have been fortunate enough to know. I..."

"Son," Joseph said, holding up his hand to halt the young man's practiced spiel. "You are wasting your well-rehearsed speech on us if you're looking for work. You've come to the wrong place. You may be the smartest, most experienced fellow in the state but we're not hiring. Sorry. If you're hungry, we can give you a hot meal, but we're just poor farmers trying to scratch out a living."

The young man jerked off his hat, took a deep

breath, and started again. "Sir, if this glorious piece of property belongs to you, then you are far from poor. Any man would consider himself wealthy to find himself the owner of such a house and fertile-looking land. I would feel blessed if you could just provide me with a meal a day, and a corner of the barn for a hard day's work. I will start before dawn and will not slow up until after dark.

"I can chop wood, plow fields, clean barns, mend fences, plant crops, repair what needs repairing, and mend and fix most anything. I can groom horses, feed cows, paint buildings, and carry water. There is nothing I won't do for a meal a day, and a roof over my head at night.

"I have been traveling this country for many months, and am willing to do anything for a chance to stay in one place for a spell. All I need is a chance to prove to you that you need me. I understand you folks are just starting out, but with an extra pair of hands, the fields will be plowed faster, the seeds planted quicker, the crops will be in sooner, the repairs done before winter, and like I said before, all I require is one meal and a pile of hay. Don't tell me you've had a better offer lately."

He paused, his chest heaving from the rush of his speech. "Just a chance," he pleaded. "I really need work, sir. You won't be sorry. Let me stay for a while, and if you are not satisfied with my work, then I'll leave without a word, I promise. Please, a trial period? I'll work hard."

"Are you from around here, son?" Clayton asked.

"No, sir, I'm from Charleston. My father came cross country from California, and met my mother along the way. My pa and me call Charleston our home. He and my grandpa were both gamblers, but that ain't the life I wanna live—in the money one day and poor the next. I want that dollar in my hand to be the result of something I did, not by flipping a nickel and having a man's bad choice put his hard earned money in my pocket." Daniel shifted his weight from one foot to the other.

Joseph and Clayton remained silent, both staring past the young man, across the road seeming to contemplate the situation.

"Thank you for your time, gentlemen, I'll be on my way." The young man put on his hat, jerked the front brim, nodded, and turned to leave.

Daniel stuck out his hand toward Clayton and nodded at Joseph. "Sirs, I do appreciate you both taking time away from your busy day to listen to me. I hope you and your family have a good year." He started back down the drive.

"Son, I'm Clayton Wilkins. This here is Joseph Martin, my father-in-law. What did you say your name was?"

Daniel Jones' heart skipped a beat at the call of his name. Now he turned and walked back.

"Daniel, sir, Daniel Jones," he paused and stood, unmoving.

"Well, Daniel," Clayton drawled, "we'll give you a try, and then we'll see. There will be three meals a day and a warm place to stay. You're right about there being a lot of repairs that need to be done around here before winter. The spring house needs to be rebuilt, the barn roof needs patching, and there's a lot of wood that needs cutting.

"There's a room in back of the barn you can use. Go ahead and store your gear in there, and then come to the kitchen door at the back of the house.

Irene, my mother-in-law, will fix you something to eat. Then you can get started but be assured young man, this is hard work.

"By the end of the trial period, if you, or I, decide this isn't the life for you, then we'll just part company with a shake of the hand and no bad feelings, fair enough?"

"Fair enough," Daniel practically shouted, and reached for Clayton's hand.

~ * ~

"Irene, where are you?" Clayton called, opening the screen door, escorting Daniel in.

Irene hurried into the kitchen and stopped suddenly at the sight of the strange young man.

"This is Daniel Jones, and he'll be helping us out a bit for a while. We're going to fix him up a room in the barn."

"Are you from around here, Mister Jones?" Irene asked with a frown.

"No, ma'am. I'm just out traveling, trying to find my place in the world," Daniel answered with a smile.

"Well, you found a placed filled with long hours, hard work, and little reward, I can tell you that. We don't dilly-dally around here."

"No, ma'am, I can see that."

Irene glared at Clayton, turned and went to the stove.

"Sit yourself at the table, Mister Jones, and I'll scramble some eggs to go with the leftover bacon and biscuits we had for breakfast."

"Thank you, ma'am, I'm starving."

"Thanks, Irene," Clayton said with a grateful smile.

"When you get through, boy, come on out and

I'll get you started."

"Yes, sir, thank you, sir."

~ * ~

After he had eaten, Daniel went outside, rolled up his sleeves, and took the lumber, hammer, and nails Clayton gave him, and headed to the spring house to start on repairs there.

While he was out, Irene and Sarah set up one of the old cots from a storage room in the barn, and found a small table and chair to fit. They made up the bed for Daniel, and placed an oil lamp on the table, along with some clean wash cloths and towels, and an enameled wash bowl.

For the rest of the morning Daniel ripped rotten boards from the spring house, hammered all the salvageable nails straight, stacked the unusable wood in a burn pile, and sanded the remaining boards free of flaking paint and dirt.

At lunchtime, Little Clay hollered for Daniel to come over to a shady table by the big sycamore tree. Little Clay placed a tray of sliced ham, with slabs of homemade bread, tomatoes, and cucumbers on the side, on the table.

When Daniel reached the tree, he was handed a large canning jar filled with chilled sweet tea, which he tilted up and guzzled steadily until it was empty. Little Clay laughed, took the jar and ran back to the house to refill it.

With a full stomach, Daniel lounged around in the shade for about half an hour before returning to the springhouse.

The rest of the day went along as usual. The men worked, Little Clay raked the chicken pen and barn, and Irene and the girls continued to work in the house, dusting, arranging, and polishing.

At suppertime, Clayton sent Clay Jr. to take Daniel's plate to him in the barn. He took the tray loaded with beef stew, several slices of fresh baked bread dripping with butter, a tin container of hot coffee, along with a spoon, cup, and napkin.

"You're gonna love this stew," Little Clay said, bending over the bowl and inhaling deeply. "My momma used to fix stew like this, and she taught Sarah how. Don't it smell good?"

"Yes, it does, but my opinion don't count today. I'm hungry enough to eat a bear—fur and all."

Little Clay giggled and backed out of the room.

"Just leave the tray outside your door on that barrel and I'll get it later, okay?"

"You bet. Thanks for bringing it. Hope it wasn't any trouble."

"Aw, you ain't no trouble, Daniel. I like having you here."

Daniel smiled and watched the boy turn and race back to the house. Taking a deep breath, he picked up his spoon and scooped up a steaming mouthful of stew. Little Clay was right, the stew was delicious. Biting into a slice of bread, he stopped chewing and listened. He could hear laughter from the kitchen. The girls' voices were musical, and he smiled at the comfort in the apparent joy in this home.

He had met Irene and Clay Jr. his first trip to the kitchen but the girls were not around. Later that day, he spotted them peeking at him from the upstairs windows while he worked on the spring house. He understood Irene's caution but hoped they would all relax around him soon. He had a mission, and he didn't want suspicious, spying eyes on him every minute. He would have to convince them to trust him, and then he could continue his grandfather's quest.

He took out a diamond studded, solid gold, heart-shaped key fob on a chain, and fingered it tenderly.

"I found it, Grandpa, I just know it. I've done the research carefully, and this has to be the place. Don't you worry none, Grandpa. I'll finish what you started. I'll find your gold, I promise."

Daniel pulled off his boots, socks, and shirt and went out to the water trough. He pumped the handle until fresh cold water poured from the spout, and washed his face, arms, and chest, and rinsed off his feet. He returned to his room and fastened the door. After stepping from his work pants, Daniel stretched out on the cot, pulled the watch fob out, and fingered it as he stared at the ceiling.

His quest to recover his grandfather's gold had been an obsession with him for so long, he felt almost uncomfortable to be so close, and know it was still unreachable. Nevertheless, he had to be patient. Still, he was uneasy. He couldn't put his finger on the reason, but figured it was just nerves.

The night was cool and peaceful. Daniel listened to the sounds of the shuffling of horse hooves, the song of crickets, and the calling of a few night birds. He stuck the chain back into his shirt and blew out the lamp. It would be too easy to fall asleep tonight. For one thing, he was exhausted. He wasn't used to hard work. For another thing, the night seemed to want to serenade him, and he wasn't going to complain. Still, he had just one more thing to do before he could sleep—just one more thing.

It was close to ten o'clock when Daniel saw

the last light extinguished in the house, and near midnight before he felt confident enough to begin his exploration of the grounds of Eagle Creek Farm without being discovered.

~ * ~

By the time Clayton and Joseph had dressed and entered the kitchen for breakfast, they could hear the hacking sound of wood being chopped out back. Joseph stood at the door, watching Daniel split and stack the wood, while Sarah and Irene dished up ham and eggs.

"He's already eaten, brought in the eggs, let the cow out to pasture, and started on the wood pile," Sarah said, sneaking a quick glance out the window. "Looks to me like he's trying to make a good impression on his first full day here."

"We're going to start on the back fields to-day. They should be ready for fall seedlings by next week or so," Clayton said, scooping a spoonful of eggs into his mouth.

"So soon? I thought you said it wouldn't be ready till next month?" Irene said.

She sat down with a cup of coffee and smiled at Mary and little Clay, who staggered into the room, trying to rub the sleep from their eyes. She and Joseph had always been early risers, and Clayton woke bright-eyed and bushy-tailed, ready for the day. Although Sarah usually woke at dawn, it took Mary and Clay Jr. an hour or so to shake the night's sleep from their minds. Early mornings were not their cup of tea.

"Well, if Daniel's gonna cut wood and repair the barn, we can concentrate on plowing the fields. You and the girls can get started on the side garden, and maybe Daniel can help you there, too."

Irene nodded and stared out the door.

"The other day I noticed a stand of pecan trees over along the left side of the back pasture, and a few hickory trees. The girls can see if there's any nuts left to gather. There're also some healthy lookin' persimmon trees too. But don't pick those until after the first frost. They won't be fit to eat until then," Irene said, pointing out toward the copse of trees in the distance. She poured coffee all around and looked at her son-in-law.

"Clayton, I asked about the school when we were in town. Mrs. Barker said it would start late September after planting season, and is located at the edge of town. How are the children going to get back and forth? It took over half an hour to get to Sycamore Grove by wagon. That's just too far to walk."

"It was going to be a surprise but Joseph and I found that buggy the blacksmith mentioned. It was in a shed behind the barn. It's in good shape, and I don't think Sarah will have a bit of trouble driving it into town.

"Then Sarah can focus on her school work, and not have to worry about the house and young'uns. I'm sure Mister O' Day, the blacksmith, will care for the horse at his stables until school is out. That is, if he doesn't charge too much."

"I can't tell you how that relieves my mind. I've been worrying about that since we arrived. I wanted so much for Sarah to just be a school girl again. By the way, is the smokehouse in good condition? Little Clay asked if you were going hunting anytime soon. We do need to get some meat smoked for the fall." Irene rose and began clearing the table.

Joseph stood, drained the last of his coffee

and stretched. "The smokehouse is ready to be filled. Clayton found some wild hog tracks the other day, and we've seen several flocks of ducks coming in over at the pond. Soon as the fields are sown, we'll go out and see what we can find. I think before long, we'll have plenty of hog, quail, venison, and squirrel to eat. I hope to get a couple of turkeys for the holidays, too."

"Excuse me, Mister Wilkins," Daniel said from the doorway. "Would it be all right if I took one of the horses into the woods? I could down a few more trees for lumber, and get it pulled home by dark."

"Can I go with him, Pa, can I? I'll be careful and won't get in his way, I promise. Can I?" Little Clay begged, bouncing in front of his father.

"You can go with Papa Joe and me to mend fences, son. You can hand us the nails," Clayton answered.

"But I'd rather go in the woods, Pa. You won't let me go alone, and I'll be with Mister Jones. Please, Pa?" he pleaded.

"I don't mind if the boy comes with me, Mister Wilkins." Daniel smiled. "I'd be glad for the company. I'll keep my eye on him, never fear."

"If you're sure..."

"Thank you, Pa, thank you. I'll help harness ol' Turk. He's a good one for pulling, he is."

"I'll fix you a bucket with some bread and jam for lunch, and a jar of water," Irene said. "Hard work makes young men hungry."

"Mister Jones, make sure Clay Jr. is nowhere near a falling tree. He's quick as a fox and you must watch him like a hawk." Sarah went to her little brother. "You mind what Mister Jones says, you hear?"

"Sarah, you make us sound like wild critters talking 'bout foxes 'n hawks. We'll be working men, and I know to stay away when a tree comes down," Clay Jr. said, and pinched his lips tightly together, intending to give her a mean frown."

"Mister Jones..."

"Don't you worry, miss. Before it's ready to fall, I'll make sure he's far away, and I can see him clearly," Daniel assured her. "And please, call me Daniel."

"Very well, Daniel, but I know my little brother, and you must take a firm hand with him."

Clayton pushed his son toward the door, and handed Daniel the lunch bucket Irene finished preparing.

"Go while you can. I hear another safety speech coming on."

"Papa," Sarah said, her face flushing.

"Honey, Little Clay is no longer a baby but as long as we treat him so, he cannot become a young man. You must let him off the leash once in a while, and let him be adventurous, or he'll do it behind your back," Clayton said, patting his daughter's arm.

A knock on the door interrupted the lecture, and Sarah ran to let Lillian in.

"Hey, y'all, I'm dressed for work. What's on the agenda for the day?"

Lillian stood at the door, wearing a pair of tan pants and a pale green shirt, her sleeves rolled up to the elbow.

"I know y'all are working folks, and I'm ready for my assignment," Lillian said.

Irene gave Lillian a hug. "It's good to see you. I hate you thinking all we do is work but I'm afraid you're right. We'll be getting a fall garden ready for some root vegetables for winter."

"I love working in the garden. You must come by and see what I've done around Uncle Williams' place. I'm ready to start whenever you are."

Lillian glanced at Clayton, who had jumped up when she entered the room. He stood by his chair, and she flashed him a bright, cheery smile. He returned Lillian's smile with a faint blush to his cheeks.

"Good morning, ma'am, nice to see you again," Clayton said.

"One more cup of coffee and we'll be ready," Irene said, noticing the look that passed between Clayton and Lillian.

"Oh, I insist you stay for dinner. I have chicken soup simmering on the stove. I'm going to fix a big pan of cornbread and some bread pudding. There will be plenty for everyone. You will stay, won't you?"

"I'd be honored to eat with y'all. Thanks."

~ FIVE ~
Guess Who Else is Coming to Dinner

Once the horse was harnessed, Daniel and
Clay Jr. walked him into the woods, looking for the
right size trees to down for firewood and lumber.

"Pa says you're from Charleston. Was it nice?
Where did you live? How come you came here? Do
your folks still live in Charleston? When...?"

"Whoa, young feller, just throw me one question at a time. Tell you what. You ask me a question,
I'll answer it, then I'll ask you a question, and you'll
answer it. Sound fair?" Daniel laughed and mussed
the boy's hair.

"Sorry, I guess that wasn't very polite. I get
confused sometimes about what's proper and what's
not," Clay Jr. said, grinding the toe of his shoe into
the leaves. "Sarah's always fussin' at me 'bout
that."

"You're just curious that's all—me, too. Go
ahead. You go first," Daniel said with a grin.

"Okay. Why did you leave Charleston?" he
asked.

"I grew up there, saw all there was to see,
and wondered what there was over the next hill,
started out one day and here I am," he said, spreading his arms wide.

"How old..." Little Clay started.

"Uh-uh," Daniel said shaking his head, "my
turn."

Clay laughed. "Sorry."

"Let's keep this question session just between
you and me, okay?"

When Clay nodded, Daniel asked, "How did
your pa come to get this house? Did he inherit it?"

"Nope, he lost his job, saw an auction posted at the bank, and bid on it. Guess nobody wanted it, so we got it. Sure was lucky, too, 'cause the house we were living in got sold at the same time, and we wouldn't have no place to live." Clay stopped by a tree and pointed. "Is this a good one?"

"That one is fine—your turn."

"How old were you when you left home? Were you scared?" the boy asked.

"I was fifteen. My pa had just died and, like you, I didn't have any place to live. I sold what he owned and took off. I was a little scared, I guess, but there were a lot of people tramping the road, so it wasn't so bad."

"Sorry 'bout your pa," Clay said, his face drooping slightly.

"Thanks, son, that's behind me now. Do you or your family know anything about the woman who lived here?"

Little Clay helped Daniel tie off Turk and watched him pull out the axe.

"Wasn't no woman, Mister Jones. It was a man. His name was Mack Kaymey. They said he had been a miner in California. He lived alone and didn't care for visitors."

He scooted back several feet while Daniel took aim and swung the axe.

"He wasn't married or had children?" Daniel asked, after prying the axe loose.

"It was my turn," Clay said.

"Well, was he?" Daniel asked crossly.

"They said he lived all by himself... then he died. Wasn't no mention of a wife or kids."

Daniel took a deep breath. "It *was* your turn, wasn't it? I got mixed-up. You can ask two questions,

80

okay?" He smiled and continued to slice at the tree.

"Okay," Clay said, brightening.

"Where are you going from here... across the west all the way to California?"

Little Clay looked up, saw Daniel pointing to the right, and then he jerked his head away from the tree. Little Clay turned and scrambled over some brush, and around some small saplings. He went behind a large tree and peeked out.

Daniel went to the other side of the tree and continued chopping. He took two angled cuts out of it, then moved to the back and pushed. First there came a creaking sound, then a crack, and with a moan, the tree began to slowly tilt, then gathered speed, and fell to the ground with a crash.

They chopped down two more, and the rest of the day was spent trimming limbs off the three fallen trees, and hooking them to chains attached to the trace on the harness.

After a break of bread and jam, Daniel and Little Clay started home. They were almost to the clearing when a growling voice from the bushes stopped them short.

"Whut've we got here—low-down, rotten poachers?"

Frank and Nate Owens stood at the edge of the woods, a sneer on their faces, a shotgun held loosely in Frank's curved arm.

Daniel reached out and slowly forced Little Clay behind him. He smiled brightly and held both arms out to his side.

"No sir, we're just taking some wood back to the house, that's all. No need to get excited. It's all legal. I work for Mister Wilkins and I'm cutting firewood today," Daniel drawled slowly.

"That's a lie," Nate said, spittle flying from his mouth. "He said he warn't hirin' nobody, we heerd it from his own mouth."

"It's not a lie," Clay Jr. cried. "My pa hired Mister Jones yesterday. He knows we're out here, so you go on and leave us alone, or you'll be in big trouble."

"O-o-o-h, hear that, Nate? We're gonna be in big trouble if we don't leave them alone. Now boy, you done gone and scared us near to death. I 'spect we's gonna have nightmares tonight, ain't we, Nate?" Frank snickered, cowered down, and his eyes slid from side to side, pretending to be frightened.

"That's right, brother, we's a'shakin' in our boots. Now, boy, you shouldn't go 'round bullyin' folks. I think we better string 'em both up, don't you?" Nate slapped his knee at what he thought was a good joke.

"I have a suggestion," Daniel said with a smirk. "Since neither one of you has the sense God gave a rock, why don't you put down that gun, and show me that your smart mouth isn't your strongest talent? Can you back up your threats, or is talking all you can do?"

"Shoot him, Frank," Nate screamed, his face twisted with rage, as he jumped from foot to foot. "Shoot him!"

"You want to do that, Frank?" Daniel asked, his voice dripping sarcasm. "You want to shoot a ten-year-old boy and an unarmed man? I thought you were a man, Frank. Are you a man, or a coward who needs a gun to fight his battles for him?"

"You watch the boy, Nate. I'll take care of this," Frank snarled.

He leaned his gun against a nearby tree,

rolled up his sleeves, and spat viciously on the ground.

Frank slowly danced toward Daniel, hopping from foot to foot, while curling his hands into fists, sticking them out in front of him.

Daniel slid his arm slowly behind him, and slipping under the back of his vest, he pulled a revolver from his belt.

"Step away from the gun, Frank," Daniel said in a quiet, no-nonsense voice.

"Hey, you cheated," Nate said hoarsely, raising his hands, and stepping back.

Frank looked dumbfounded and froze in his tracks.

"Frank, tell your brother to step back," Daniel warned, pulling back the hammer of the gun.

"Get back, stupid. He's got the drop on us." Frank reached over and hit Nate in the face with the back of his upraised hand.

"You gonna let him get away with that?" Nate whined.

"What'd ya want me to do, idjit, git shot?" His brother grumbled.

"Clay, get on the horse," Daniel ordered. "You two yee-haws, git," he shouted, and fired the gun at their feet.

Nate and Frank Owens danced back a few steps, turned and scrambled through the underbrush. Daniel grabbed the shotgun that Frank left, and stuck his pistol back into his belt. He grabbed the lead strap from the horse's halter, hoisted Clay onto the horse, and started back to the house.

Neither one spoke a word on the trip back, and when they reached the backyard, Clay Jr. slipped off Turk's back, bolted for the house and disappeared into the kitchen.

Daniel unhooked the chains from the harness, and dropped the logs off before leading Turk to the barn. He rubbed the horse down, poured a small can of oats into the wooden trough, and forked some hay into the stall. When Clayton entered, followed by a worried looking Joseph, Daniel looked up, and saw Lillian wasn't far behind.

"Heard you had some trouble in the woods?" Clayton asked, frowning.

He reached into his back pocket and began wiping his hands with the rag he always kept there.

"Wasn't nothing for you to worry about," Daniel said, pitching a second fork of hay into the stall.

"It is when it concerns the safety of my son. Little Clay said it was the Owens boys, and they accused you of trespassing and kidnapping?"

"I don't think they really intended to do any harm. It was just a scare tactic. You know, snarling like scared wolves or bluffing dogs. Maybe a little pushing and shoving, just trying to scare us. I shouldn't have pulled my gun, but I didn't want Little Clay to get hurt in the scuffle.

"I probably could have handled them, but they're not very smart, and it's hard to second guess stupid. Anyway, I don't think they'll be back," he said nonchalantly, and hung the pitchfork on a nail.

Lillian stepped up beside Clayton. "Those Owens boys have been bullies since they were old enough to make a fist. They were in the second and third grade when I started school, but the teacher couldn't handle them. They stood in the corner for misbehaving, or were expelled for fighting every other day.

"Reverend Talley said one Sunday that there

is good in the worst of us, but I'm not sure he ever met Frank or Nate. If he had, he might change his tune, or sermon, that is. You're right to carry a gun around here, Daniel. Clayton, you and Joseph might be wise to do the same." She cocked her head toward Clayton.

Joseph stuck his hands in his pockets. "You may be right, Lillian. I've a mind to tell the mayor anyway. They don't have reason to be on our land. They're the ones trespassing. I'm sure when they saw you were working here, son, it just riled 'em some, and they got mad that Clayton hadn't hired them. To be perfectly honest, we wouldn't have hired those ruffians even if we had plenty of money. Wouldn't trust them two anymore than I'd kiss a rattlesnake."

Joseph pinched his fingers together and jabbed his hand forward imitating a striking snake.

"How come you were carrying a gun?" Clayton asked, focusing on Daniel.

"Well, sir, I don't know these woods, and I wasn't sure what we might run into. Just didn't want to take a chance, that's all. Was I wrong?" He stood still, returning Clayton's steady gaze.

They looked into each other's eyes for a second or two, then Clayton smiled, and stuck his hand out.

"Thank you for taking care of my son, Daniel. He told me how you pushed him behind you, and later helped him get on ol' Turk's back. You're a good man, Daniel. I'd be proud to have you join us at our table for meals."

Daniel's face flushed, he smiled, and slowly nodded. "I'm obliged to your kind words, Mister Wilkins. I'd like that."

"Forget the wood for now. Better go bring the cows up to the corral. Don't want to give those Owen brothers any temptations."

"Little Clay said you took their gun. Is that so?" Joseph looked around.

"Yes sir, I did. It's right there by the door. Thought you might want to return it by way of the mayor. It wouldn't hurt to let him know what's going on. Without proof, it's just my word against theirs," Daniel said.

"You forget about Little Clay," Clayton said with a wry grin. "He'll be telling that story over and over for some time to come. I'm sure it would cheer him considerable to get to tell the mayor. Of course, those Owens boys get taller with each telling, and that shotgun gets bigger. You—well, you just get tougher and tougher. The way he remembers it, when you pulled your gun, those boys started shaking and crying with fear." He chuckled.

Daniel laughed out loud, and Joseph grinned at the picture Little Clay painted for his Grandma and sisters.

"I don't recall it exactly that way," Daniel said with a chuckle. "The gun surprised 'em all right, and I guess when I fired near their feet, it did speed up their decision to leave, but they weren't shaking or begging, I guarantee. They were mad as hornets, and I expect they'll be trying to think up something we won't like."

"I figured that much and you're probably right. They'll just deny they were ever in the woods, and if they swear they weren't there, then that gun couldn't be theirs, could it?" Joseph said. "You keep the shotgun. Being out in the barn, you'll be the first to hear trouble."

"I do thank you, Daniel. After you bring in the cows, come on up to the house and wash up. The ladies are frying up some chicken, and if I'm not mistaken, the scents coming from the kitchen can only mean one thing, Irene's fixing her famous bread pudding. Trust me, you don't won't to be late for that." Clayton grinned. "You're in for a treat, too, Lillian," Clayton added.

"No, sir," Daniel said with a smile. "I won't be late."

~ SIX ~
A Glimpse into the Past

Sarah tossed and turned for almost an hour before throwing back her covers and lit a small candle to light her way down the staircase. She had been thinking of the incident Little Clay talked about all afternoon and throughout supper. It was the first time she had seen Daniel up close for any length of time, and although he seemed quiet and polite when she first met him, tonight she noticed how handsome he was. He was also soft spoken, and she had a hard time imagining him pulling a gun, and driving off two rough bullies.

She wandered into the library and lit one of the wall lamps. Walking slowly along the rows of books, her fingers trailed over the spines of the books. She stopped and tilted her head in order to read some of the titles. The wavering flames flickered off the gold lettering of a leather bound book that drew her attention. Slipping it out, she ran her hand over the soft cover. *Jane Eyre*, she read softly. She held the book close to her, blew out the lamp, picked up her candle, and headed back to her room.

Sarah threw her robe over the foot of her bed, and slipped off her house shoes. After snuggling under her quilts, she moved the candle closer, and opened the book for a good read.

She flipped the cover over and saw the title page, Jane Eyre, written by Charlotte Bronte, published 1847. She shivered in anticipation and turned the page. She stopped, confused, and flipped the page back, and then forward again. The second page was not printed. It was handwritten in a graceful, feminine script. She quickly turned several more pages and found they were all handwritten. She went back to the first handwritten page and began reading.

After much thought and deliberation, I have decided to put pen to paper to record the months I spent disguised as a man so that when I'm gone, my story might be known. I have chosen this particular book cover, Jane Eyre, to disguise my journal since the author, Charlotte Bronte, had to use a man's name to hide her gender in order to have her first piece published, and I used a man's appearance to hide mine.

Charlotte Bronte published her first poems under the name of Currer Bell and I, Aimee McKay, lived under the name of Mack Kaymey, a slight scrambling of letters that gave me my new name. I had no choice.

Over a year ago, and I must interject that it seems like a lifetime ago, I ran away, under the cloak of darkness, from a loving father and brother to marry, I thought, a man who loved me. He did not. Unmarried, beaten down and abandoned, I sold the last piece of jewelry that belonged to my dear, departed mother, to sail from San Francisco to New York, find a job, and start a new life.

I was twenty-one, dishonored, penniless, and ashamed. I prayed for a way to prevent my family from ever learning of the disgrace I had brought upon them.

We transferred to the S.S. Central America in Panama. The ship was later seriously damaged in a hurricane and was sinking.

A dear old man I had befriended, confided to me that he could not swim, and knew he would not survive the high waves of the sea. He insisted I take his money belt and leather bag, both were filled with gold.

Along with the other women and children, I was placed into a lifeboat and rescued by the ship, Ellen, that delivered us to Charleston. There, I cut off my hair, bought clothes, changed my name, and began a new life under the guise of a gold miner from California.

I feared every day would bring about a familiar face that would scream, "Imposter!" A face that would reveal to the world that I was a liar and a fraud. The sound of every horse approaching caused a pain in my chest. How long could I fool the world?

Now, would you believe that a fellow passenger I met on the disastrous voyage bought the property next to mine?

His name is Lucas Chase, and he is a successful miner who made his fortune in the gold fields. I must admit, he is a handsome fellow and seems to have a very pleasant nature. I wanted him to keep his distance, but that wasn't to be. He saved me from an encounter with a vicious poacher, and when I fainted, he discovered my true identity. He told me he had been looking for me, and that I could count on him to keep my secret.

They are building my house, my hide-a-way. The magnificent turtle shell in which I will hide myself away for the rest of my days, if I have to, grieving for my family, regretting

*my past indiscretions, and punishing myself
for the sinful decisions that would destroy my
family and my life. At twenty-one, I feel like
an old woman, sad, used up, and lonely, and
that hiding is the only fitting retribution I
feel I deserve.*

Sarah sat stunned, and reluctantly looked
away from the page. She placed a ribbon between
the pages to mark her place, and slowly closed the
book. With tears in her eyes, she looked around the
room with a new perspective. Aimee McKay, alone
and living a lie, had walked through these rooms,
touched this furniture, despaired over her past and
her future, and faced a life where she feared every
moment she would be discovered.

After blowing out the candle, Sarah debated
whether to tell her family about the journal. She decided she would finish reading it first, and then decide. She lay there drifting off, and heard the
strange howl they had all heard a couple of weeks
before. She jumped up and peered through the curtains.

She saw Daniel standing shirtless in front of
the barn, shotgun ready. He crept along the outside
of the barn and stared into the woods. He turned
and walked to the other side, and then disappeared
into the shadows.

She quietly raised her window and heard voices directly beneath her. She looked down and saw
Papa Joe and Pa heading toward the barn. Daniel
came around the corner and shrugged when he saw
them, and all three quietly walked toward the
chicken coop. A few minutes later, they returned,
and Daniel went back into the barn. Sarah heard the

side door close as her grandfather and father returned to their beds.

Her third attempt to sleep was more successful than her first two. She smiled as she drifted off. Sarah had hated the idea of moving here. Thoughts of boredom once filled her head, but boredom proved to be the last thing she would have to worry about.

~ * ~

Daniel pulled off his trousers and fell back on his cot. He ran his fingers through his hair, and over his face, and felt the medallion warm against his skin. The cool air cleared his mind and let him breathe deeply. These people were good, hard-working people, and not knowing what to expect, this family had been a surprise. Daniel had spent the past few years devising a plan that would allow him to locate the place his grandfather had talked about before he died.

However, these nice people had not been included in his plan, and now he felt uneasy. Peering into every corner, Daniel found nothing. He heard the sounds of the horses as they moved around in their stalls, and saw the cows standing in the corral, swishing their tails in unison.

Getting out of bed, he went to the barn door, and stared at the house. All was quiet. He started to turn away when one of the upstairs windows caught his eye. A soft glow faded away. Someone had just blown out a candle or lamp. The dark house loomed before him, and seemed to be watching him. Backing slowly into the shadows, his eyes fixed on the house, and he began to feel guilty for something he hadn't yet done. Daniel turned, walked determinedly back to his room, and fell onto his bed. Smiling, he closed his eyes and fell asleep, holding the gold watch fob between his fingers.

~ * ~

The next morning, after a thorough search of the surrounding woods, everyone returned to their normal routines. Joseph and Clayton took both horses into the field directly behind the house to continue plowing. Daniel cut the smaller sections of the fallen trees into firewood, and cleaned up the larger portions to be split into rough boards to repair the barn and chicken house. Mary gathered eggs, and Little Clay turned the cows into the pasture, while Sarah worked with Irene in the small garden near the kitchen.

It was Clay Jr. who first saw Isaac and Albert crossing the field. Albert waved, hollered and ran toward the house. As Clay Jr. ran to meet him, he saw movement in the high grass behind him.

"Pa," he called to his father. "It's Mister Washington and Albert."

Clayton paused, wiped his face, and wrapped the reins around the plow handle. He nodded to Joseph and started toward Isaac.

Isaac stuck out his hand and shook Clayton's. A frown and a furrowed brow illustrated his worry.

"Morning, Mister Wilkins. We won't take up much of your time, but I feels this is important. My boy, Macon, was at the general store yesterday and heard them Owens boys spoutin' off about somethin' that happened in your woods. Now, I know it ain't none of my business but them boys ain't nobody to trifle with. They's easily riled up, mean, got too much time on their hands, and takes great pleasure in makin' trouble. You just might need somethin' to kinda even the odds."

Isaac glanced down at the dog they brought, and ran his hand over the animal's head.

"Mister Kaymey bought several fine English setters to use as hunting dogs and guard the house. Down through the years that line has produced some right smart dogs. In fact, he gave me a pair of fine pups the first Christmas he was here."

Isaac paused, looked across the field and smiled. He glanced up and saw everyone looking at him.

"Sorry, I was thinking 'bout when I first saw my pups.

"We don't breed them but every three years or so. This here is Honey. One of my baby girls named her when she was a pup on account of them yellow eyes. Now, don't let the name fool you. She's powerful smart and protective.

"She's young enough to be trained to your likin', and I don't think there'll be nothin' sneakin' up on you, day or night, with Honey around. We'd be mighty proud if you'd accept her as a gift from our house to yours. She'll be gentle to those she loves but a powerful enemy to those what threatens her territory. She's also familiar with the woods."

Clayton squatted down and took the dog's head in his hands. The animal squirmed with happiness. Her long, wet tongue lapped joyfully at Clayton's face, and she offered her paw to her new owner.

"Oh, Pa, she's grand. She's the most wonderfulest, most beautifullest dog I ever saw," Little Clay gushed.

"Don't think I've ever heard a dog described quite like that," Isaac said and laughed. "Mister Wilkins..."

"Please, Isaac, no more Mister Wilkins. It's Clayton—please," he said, offering his hand.

"Clayton," Isaac nodded, shaking hands. "I think y'all gonna rest easier once Honey gets settled in. Looks like she knows this is her new home already."

"This is a fine welcoming gift, Isaac. I'd be proud to have a handsome animal like this to guard my family, and there's no doubt, she'll come in handy at hunting time. I thank you, friend. Thank you very much."

They watched the blue-gray, yellow-eyed dog trot around the field and make her way, nose down to the ground, to the backyard. After sniffing around the area, she headed for the water trough and began lapping up the cool liquid. When she finished, she stretched out in the shade and rested her head across her paws. Little Clay and Albert ran to the spot, and sat on either side of her, stroking her shiny fur.

"I'll let you get back to work, Mis... Clayton. I've got a day of weedin' ahead of me. If you need me for anything, just send your boy, or fire three shots in the air. We'll hear and come quick as we can. You take care now." They shook hands and he called to his son.

"Albert, you got chores, boy. We gotta get back home. You two can play another time."

Albert groaned, got up, and gave Honey the order to stay. He waved to Little Clay and ran to catch up with his father.

~ * ~

Sarah was glad Clay had the dog. She wasn't an animal lover, but she had seen her little brother moping around when there was no one to play with. This dog was the perfect answer. She made a mental note to fix something nice for Albert's family to show her appreciation.

After they finished the gardening, Sarah asked if she was needed further. When told she could go, she ran upstairs, grabbed Aimee's journal and took off for the orchard.

Sarah found the grove of peach trees shortly after they had arrived, and decided it was her favorite place to be alone. There were twelve large trees, and she loved the quiet, peaceful area. She settled down on the grass, leaned against one of the trees, took a deep breath, and opened the book.

> *I'm getting ahead of myself. I'm not much of a writer, so I beg the reader's indulgence as I attempt to pen my story and only hope that in doing so, I paint you a picture in words.*
>
> *As soon as we docked in Charleston, I quickly melted into the crowd on the wharf. In my damp and bedraggled state, it was not hard to wander unnoticed among the lesser known streets of Charleston, and purchase second-hand clothing from discount stores. In a cheap bath house, I chopped off my hair, dressed in two pairs of oversized trousers, two shirts, and crammed a misshapen hat over my poorly hacked hair.*
>
> *I bought a half-starved cart horse, saddle, and a pack mule from a livery stable, loaded up, and started my journey west. I discovered this lovely town, made dear friends with Ernest Gaines, the banker,*

bought some land and a cabin. Later, I hired an architect to build my house so I could settle down.

I discovered a group of people living, or rather, hiding, in the woods of my new property and upon their discovery, made more new friends. They were Rose and Albert Washington, their son Isaac, and several friends. They were escaped slaves, and warm, generous people. I helped some of them find the Underground Railroad, and created papers for the Washingtons, and the others, who wanted to remain here.

Isaac is a lively, adventurous boy, who is a constant joy in my life. He loves to play hide and seek, but his favorite game is 'Pirate's Treasure', a game we play over and over. He will hide a box and leave clues to lead me to the treasure when it is my turn, and I do the same.

Rose discovered I am not who, or what, I seem. Yet she never reveals my secret. I owe my friends, for after all, I have kept their secret, and I know they will keep mine. As a woman, it is only natural to crave another woman's company, and it was comforting to be myself now and then.

Sarah closed the book. She tried to picture Aimee cutting off her beautiful, silken hair, dressing in layers of used, bulky men's clothing, and speaking in a low, coarse male voice. How hard it would have been, never allowing herself to make an error, slip, or falter.

She struggled even harder to picture Isaac,

the tall serious, hard-working father of Albert, ever being an energetic, boisterous young child who loved playing hide and seek, or searching for an imaginary pirate's treasure. The very thought made her laugh out loud.

"What are you laughing about?" Little Clay asked. He and Honey fell on the ground beside her. "Was it something funny in that book? Whatcha readin'?"

Sarah shoved the book under the edge of her skirt.

"Why aren't you helping Pa and Papa Joe?" She asked quickly, trying to take her little brother's mind off the book.

"Why aren't *you* helping Grandma?" He asked, imitating Sarah's voice.

"That's none of your business. What do you want?" Sarah scrambled to her feet, holding the book close.

"Is that a secret book? I betcha it is, and I bet you're not supposed to have it," Little Clay said, watching his sister with narrowed eyes.

"You want to read it? Go ahead. It's about an orphan girl who goes to work for a grand gentleman, who is raising a ward, and has a crazy wife locked in the attic, and they fall in love, but they can't marry because..."

"Stop, stop," Clay Jr. moaned. "Ugh. No, I don't want to read it. It sounds stupid. Does Gram know you have it?"

"Yes, she does. She said she wants to read it when I finish. Any other questions, smarty?" Sarah couldn't help but flinch at her white lie.

"No, and I don't care 'bout no silly girl's book. I'd rather read about a knight slaying dragons, or a pirate on the high seas."

Little Clay tilted his head at his sister, and brandished an invisible sword. He began to dance around, slashing through the air, jabbing unseen enemies. He paused when he saw her smile.

"Whatcha laughin' 'bout? What's so funny?" He said, pursing his lips, and placing his fists on his hips.

"Oh, please. Don't act foolish. I was just thinking how all little boys are alike with their thoughts of adventures and exploring." She smiled.

"What's wrong with that?" he growled.

"Nothing, Little Clay, nothing's wrong with that. It's just a boy thing, that's all."

"Don't call me Little Clay," he cried. "Just Clay, okay, just Clay."

"Oooh, Clay is it? Well, we'll see about that. Maybe if you stop acting little, we'll stop calling you *little*. Think about it."

She flipped her skirt at him, clutched the book to her chest, and headed back to the house.

~ SEVEN ~
Dreams of Yesterday

The smell of fresh baked bread filled the air, and Daniel's mouth watered. He hammered the final nail into the tin roof of the spring house, and stood back to admire his handy work. He had lied when he boasted about all his previous handyman accomplishments, when trying to convince Clayton Wilkins to hire him. However, he quickly learned that all it took to be a good handyman was determination and common sense.

They provided all the supplies, and a look around at the other buildings gave him all the instruction he needed. He placed the hammer and nails into the wooden tool box, grabbed the leather strap, and swung it over his shoulder, turning at the same time.

"Wh-u-uf," Sarah cried, colliding with Daniel.

Holding the book in one hand, she stuck her other hand behind her to break her fall. She heard a rip and found herself dangling by her sleeve, with Daniel gripping her free arm by her ripped sleeve, and pulled her upright.

"Are you two all right?" Irene called, rushing over to them. "I saw you collide."

"Don't worry. I've been hit harder by a butterfly," Daniel said and grinned.

"Nonsense, you saved her from a nasty fall. That was fast action. Sarah, are you hurt?"

Sarah's face glowed with the blush of embarrassment, as she covered her bare shoulder with the torn sleeve.

"N-n-no, just startled, that's all. Thank you, Mister Jones. I'm s-so sorry. I wasn't looking where I was going. I thought I'd hit the ground for sure." Sarah stared at the spot where she would have landed.

"Your fast actions have saved two of my grandchildren from harm. I'm very grateful, Daniel. How about some fresh bread and jam with a cup of coffee?" Irene patted Daniels's shoulder, and gave him a wide smile.

"Thank you, ma'am, my mouth's been watering from the smell of that bread all morning. Just let me put these tools back in the barn, and wash up a bit, and I'll be right there," Daniel answered, tipped his hat, and headed for the barn.

He arrived at the kitchen a few minutes later and wiped his feet thoroughly before he entered. Several loaves of fragrant, golden-crust bread sat side by side on a long table under the side windows, along with two, round, sugary cakes dusted with cinnamon.

The coffee bubbled and the tea kettle whistled when Daniel sat at the table. He heard the stomping of feet outside the door, and turned as Joseph and Clayton entered.

"Howdy, Daniel, the spring house looks fine, boy, just fine. You did a good job," Clayton said with a smile. He took off his hat and hung it on a rack by the door.

"Clayton, your daughter tore through the yard and smashed into Daniel here. If he hadn't grabbed her to keep her from falling, she could have broken something," his mother-in-law said.

She frowned and glanced at Sarah, who set cups and saucers on the table.

Before Clayton could respond, the screen door slammed and Little Clay raced in, with Honey at his heels.

"No dog in the house, Little Clay. I've warned you about that. She has to stay outside. That's the rule. I don't want to have to tell you again."

Irene grabbed Honey by the collar, led her to the door, and pushed her outside. The dog sat on the porch. Her head drooped, and she peered through the screen, her tail slowly sweeping back and forth across the wooden floor.

"Aw, Gram, look at her. She's lonely out there. She'll be good. I'll train her to sit in the corner. Please?" he begged.

"Absolutely not, houses are for people. Outdoors is for dogs. That's the way it is. No. Don't open your mouth. The dog stays outside. That's final."

She snapped her fingers and pointed to her grandson, watching his mouth open and close.

"Would you like some jam?" Sarah asked, glancing at Daniel. She placed sliced bread in front of him.

"No, thank you. I would like some butter, though, if you have plenty," he answered, smiling, looking into her eyes.

"Yes, uh, I'll get it." Turning around, she bumped into Mary, who had just walked in.

"Watch it," Mary grumbled. "You could say you're sorry."

"Sorry," Sarah said under her breath.

She took the cloth from over the bowl of butter and sat it near Daniel.

"Goodness, child," Irene chided. "Your mind must be a million miles away, running into two people in the same day. You're usually the organized one, but lately, you can't wait to rush somewhere."

"It must be that l-u-u-v story she's reading,"

smirked Clay Jr. "She's had her head stuck in it all day. Maybe she's daydreaming about the hero and wishes he was in l-u-u-v with her," he giggled.

"Gram," Sarah cried, her face flushing ever deeper.

"Clayton Wilkins, Junior, you mind your tongue. We don't go around making others feel badly. Would you like it if someone teased you about that dog?" Irene said sternly.

"No, ma'am," Little Clay said softly, furrowing his brow, and hanging his head. "I'm sorry, Sarah."

"I think reading is a fine way to pass the time. It's educational and informative. What book are you reading, Miss Sarah?" Daniel asked, buttering his steaming slice of bread without looking up.

"It's called *Jane Eyre* by Charlotte Bronte." Sarah's lie was again bitter on her tongue, even so, she went on. "It's about an orphan in England who became a governess, and took a job out in the countryside to care for a young ward."

"Sounds lovely," Irene said. "Perhaps I'll get a chance to read it this winter." She walked around the table pouring coffee into cups.

"I like books about places far away. If you can't travel, that's the way to learn about them," Daniel said.

Sarah glanced at him and nodded, but said nothing.

"Mister Wilkins, I mean, Clayton... since I've finished the spring house, what would you like me to start on next?" Daniel asked.

"Well, I thought that..." Clayton began.

"I could really use him for a while," Irene interrupted. "I know you have a lot that needs to be done, but that cellar—well, we need to clean it out for root storage and, well..." Her voice trailed off as she grimaced, and involuntarily shivered.

Clayton grinned. "Gram, I know you and Sarah have been dreading going down there. Daniel, would you mind checking it out, and seeing if it's safe? They could use you to help move stuff around and clean it out. Make sure the spider webs are brushed down. Gram is unusually fearful of spiders. You don't mind, do you, Son?"

"I'd be happy to." Daniel grinned. "Cellars are my specialty. I'll bet young Clay here could help, and Miss Sarah might supervise if she's not too busy reading. Us guys don't have any idea how a lady likes her cellar set up, do we, Clay?"

Little Clay shook his head and the frown deepened. He wiped his mouth, laid down his napkin, and gazed at his father.

"Pa?" he asked slowly, rising and going to his father's side.

Clayton blew across the top of his hot coffee, glanced up, one brow raised, while Little Clay stared at his shoes, shifting from one foot to the other.

"You got something to say, boy? Spit it out. I don't bite."

"Pa, I've been Little Clay, or Clay Junior, for as long as I can remember, and when I was little, it wasn't so bad. But Pa, I'm getting bigger now, and I like it when Daniel calls me just Clay. Now that I'm growing up, I don't want to be called Little Clay anymore. Can't you all just call me Clay?"

"Sarah says I have to stop acting little and I will, I promise. Just let my name be plain, old Clay, please? Please?"

"This is a day I've dreaded," Clayton said

slowly. "Children just don't want to stay children long enough. At least, I don't think so. Little Clay is growing up, and isn't a baby anymore. He's getting to be a young boy. It saddens me to see my babies grow up, but there's no stopping it."

Reaching into his back pocket, Clayton pulled out a handkerchief, blew his nose and took a deep breath. He stood, cleared his throat, and placed his hand on his son's head.

"I guess I knew this day would come sometime. I wasn't prepared for it to be so soon."

"Pa, you told Sarah not to treat me like a baby any more. A grown-up name might help with that," Clay Jr. added.

Clayton smiled at his anxious son. He stroked his chin for a moment, and then picked up his coffee cup.

"From now on, this boy, son of Susan and Clayton Franklin Wilkins, who is now known as Little Clay, or Clay Junior, will be addressed as Clay. Just plain, old Clay. I proclaim it."

"Thank you, Pa," Clay said solemnly.

Joseph began to clap his hands and everyone joined in.

"To Clay," Daniel cried.

"To Clay!" the group chorused.

Clay ran outside, and when he was out of earshot, his father said, "It's a happy day for Clay but it's a sad day for me." His eyes were full of emotion.

"He doesn't realize that *Little Clay* could get away with a lot more than just *Clay* can. If he wants to grow up, then more power to him," Clayton said, and smiled ruefully.

Joseph drained his cup and rose. "That field ain't getting plowed by itself, Clayton. We'd better get back."

The men left for the fields and the women began cleaning the kitchen. Daniel called Clay in to examine the cellar. Sarah tied a scarf over her hair to protect it from the dirt and dust, and put an apron on over her dress.

There were four windows high on the west wall of the cellar. Daniel pulled a box against wall, and stood on it in order to open two of them. Fresh air flowed in, and after wiping the glass, the basement was a little brighter. The other two windows had been painted over.

"Why would she paint the windows?" Sarah asked, as she fanned the dust from her nose.

"She who," Daniel asked, jerking his head around.

Sarah, stunned by her blunder, froze for a moment, and then laughed nervously.

"I don't know why I said she. I meant he, I really did, I meant *he*."

Daniel watched, as Sarah puttered around aimlessly, clearly flustered, but he didn't push the subject.

It was obvious there was more work to be done in the cellar than they could complete in one day. They organized the boxes, cleaned off the shelves, and took an old broom to sweep down most of the cobwebs, and a couple of abandoned wasp nests. As the sun moved low in the sky, it soon became too dark to work, and they decided to tackle it first thing in the morning with hot water, soap, scrub brushes and brooms.

~ * ~

That night Sarah was too tired to read. She bathed in the dressing room next to her bedroom, and practically fell into bed. She lay there wondering about Aimee.

"Which was her bedroom?" she murmured, "Did she spend much time in the library?"

She had lived here at one time or another, yet Isaac seldom spoke of her. She knew in her heart that he knew much more than he was telling.

She closed her eyes and a soft, humming melody started in her mind. She was not familiar with the tune, and reminded herself to ask her grandmother in the morning what tune she was thinking of.

"It's lovely, just lovely," she whispered, before drifting off to sleep.

~ * ~

In the barn, Daniel opened one of the double doors and peered up at the house. His muscles ached, and his eyes burned from all the dust in the cellar.

The windows were dark, except one. He knew it was Sarah's window because he had seen her spying on him when he first arrived. The light finally went out and the room was dark, along with the others.

Daniel thought of Sarah. She was so pretty and didn't even know it. He loved her shyness and... no, this was ridiculous. She was one of "them," and he couldn't think of her except as someone in the way.

He hurried back to his room and fastened the door behind him—not wanting to wake to that... that... feeling he just had. The closed door might not keep the thoughts out, but it wouldn't hurt to secure it. Jamming the chair up against the door handle, memories of today buzzed like a hornet's nest. Still, somewhere in the middle of his thoughts, Daniel fell asleep.

Slumber was fragmented with dreams and noises...

...a small cabin by a creek, the smacking sound of a hand against solid flesh, a scream, and a woman sobbing as if her heart was breaking. There was the sound of doors slamming, horse hooves pounding, and then fading. Daniel floated toward consciousness, but struggle as he might, he felt himself drifting off again. The struggle to stay awake failed.

Now, the sounds were more familiar, the fluttering, flapping sound of cards being shuffled, the clink and ching of coins hitting the table, along with gruff laughter, and the sound of money being scraped across a wooden table, then a woman's high-pitched giggle and a man's harsh laugh.

Daniel shakily pushed himself upright. His heart pounding, he staggered to his feet, splashed water on his sweating face, and took deep, gulping breaths. He sat on the side of the bed, put his head in his hands, and fought to stay awake. After a few minutes, he gave up as the fog of exhaustion engulfed him once more. When his muscles turned to jelly, he melted across the bed, and when his head touched the mattress, sleep overcame him.

Daniel became aware of the slapping sound of waves. At first it was just sounds he heard, and then a scene unfolded. A ripping sound sliced through the air when a massive sail tore loose from the rigging that attached it to the mast, and it swung back and forth over his head.

The raindrops stung like tiny pebbles against his back, and the deck bucked like a raging bull trying to throw him into the foaming sea. Hearing the sputter and coughs of a dying engine, the giant paddlewheel jerked, yanked at the sea, and then seemed to surrender to the quiet death of stillness.

Glittering debris covered the deck. Shaking the salty water from his eyes, he realized the debris was ingots, sparkling coins, and gold pieces scattered everywhere. In his mind, he saw a woman staring at the raging sea, and ignored the treasure at her feet. An old man pushed his belt and carpet bag toward her, even as she shook her head, and he could see by her body language that she was trying to refuse it.

The picture started fading away, and the scene changed. The crew began lowering women and children into the two remaining lifeboats that hadn't capsized. The woman he had seen before was slung back and forth before a crewmember took her arm, and tied a rope around her waist. The sailor forced her over the rail, and began to lower her into a waiting lifeboat.

Daniel heard a splintering sound above him, and looked up in time to see the upper half of the mast crashing down upon him.

"Eee-i-i-i-!" The cry escaped his lips, and his arms flew up protectively, and darkness enveloped him.

Opening his eyes, Daniel found himself laying crossways in his bed. His hair was damp with sweat, and he could swear he tasted sea salt.

The room was foggy and stuffy. Jerking the chair away from the door, he staggered outside.

Heading for the horse trough, he ducked his head in the water, and ran his hands through his hair. Rinsing the sweat from his arms and chest, he washed his mouth out, and went back to the barn. He turned suddenly, squinting into the dark around him. The nightmare had spooked him. Somewhere in the back of his mind, the dream had loosened a memory that had been wedged securely among other childhood recollections.

Falling once more onto the bed, Daniel slipped into a fretful sleep, with large waves chasing him, and he bumped into Sarah over and over again, and the Owen brothers yelled from the woods.

"Whut've we got here? You don't belong here... git... git."

The next morning Daniel woke late and jumped to his feet. Rubbing the sleep from his face, he staggered into the yard.

"Bad night, young feller?" Joseph asked, while pumping water into a couple of metal buckets. "You look plumb wore out, and you haven't got the sleep out of your eyes yet. Didn't you get any rest at all?"

"Nothing to worry about." Daniel stumbled to horse trough. "Sorry I'm so late."

"Ain't no skin off my nose," Joseph said, leaning against the pump. "But you'd better hurry if you want any breakfast, 'cause the women don't like to dawdle much in that hot kitchen when they got other things to do."

"I will, thanks." Daniel splashed more water on his face, dried off on his sleeve, and rushed to the house.

"Sorry I'm late, ladies. I seem to have overslept. It won't happen again, I swear," Daniel said sheepishly, standing outside. He tapped shyly on the screen door.

"Everybody's allowed one mistake." Irene smiled. "You've just had yours. Now, get in here, sit down, and eat. The rest of us have weeding to do."

"Yes, ma'am," Daniel replied. He hurried into the kitchen and took a seat at the table.

~ EIGHT ~
Aimee's Story

"Where is Little, oops, sorry. Where is Clay this morning?" Daniel asked.

"Well, sleepy head, Clay is down in the cellar getting ready to start work. Sarah gathered up a basket of rags, and Papa Joe is bringing in a couple of buckets of water so you can start cleaning those shelves." Irene motioned to the cellar door.

Daniel quickly cleaned his plate and emptied his cup. "Much obliged, Miss Irene, Miss Mary. I'd better get going. Miss Sarah's likely to sic that dog of Clay's on me if I don't."

He hopped down the cellar stairs, expecting to see Sarah and Clay busy at work. Instead, Sarah sat on the floor, a stack of newspapers in front of her, with several spread out to her side.

"Little, sorry, Clay, go get Gram. Hurry," Sarah said, her voice rising.

"What'd you find? Is it a treasure?" Daniel asked. His questions were followed by a quick laugh that sounded slightly false.

"I'm not sure but it just could be."

Sarah sat cross-legged, studying her new find. She returned his grin, but it too, looked insincere.

Sounds of footsteps interrupted Daniel's thoughts, and he moved aside to let Irene pass.

"Sarah, what is it?" Irene asked, wiping her damp hands on her apron.

"Gram, I didn't tell you before but that book Clay saw me reading wasn't *Jane Eyre*. It was a journal the previous owner wrote and put a false cover on. It tells...," Sarah glanced around, then snapped her mouth shut.

Bobbie Shafer

"It tells what, Sarah?" her grandmother asked impatiently.

"Gram, I'm sorry, but this isn't that important. I shouldn't have called you away from your chores. It'll wait. You're right, we do have things to do. I'll tell you later. I'm going to take these upstairs." Sarah rose and gathered up the papers.

"If this is private, I'll be happy to step outside," Daniel said with a forced grin, although his teeth were aching to find out what Sarah had discovered.

"No, no, it just a silly little thing I saw in the paper. I'll run these up to my room, and we can get to work."

She took the stack of papers and hurried up the stairs past her sister and Grandma.

"What's come over her?" Mary asked, peering over her grandmother's shoulder, when her sister was out of earshot.

"It's just the age, I think," Irene answered. "Sarah's not a child anymore, and she's not quite a woman. Girls her age dream of other things. She may have seen something in the paper that she wanted and just didn't know how to ask. The child knows we can't afford a single thing that isn't absolutely necessary, but that doesn't stop a body from wanting. Don't you have wishes?" Irene asked softly, stroking her youngest granddaughter's hair.

"Doesn't everybody?" Mary said with a grin.

"The good Lord made a lot more of our kind than he did the wealthy kind. We'll get our blessings in ways that money can't buy." Irene comforted her.

"Come on, Gram, let's tackle that garden."

When they left, Daniel looked at Clay.

"Hey, buddy, what in the world's going on

here? What did your sister find that excited her so?"
He smiled and tousled the boy's hair.

"Dunno," Clay mumbled.

He picked up some papers Sarah left and
stacked them on a shelf. "We were moving these
newspapers and she suddenly stopped, kinda choked
or something, and started reading. Then she began
to search through all the papers, reading some, dis-
carding others. She seemed happy, then sad, and
when you walked in, she told me to go get Gram.
That's all I know."

"Didn't she say anything... anything at all?"
Daniel asked in a soft, coaxing voice.

"Nope... yep, she did but it didn't make much
sense. She just said, "Oh, my goodness, it's true, it's
true." That's all."

"Well, maybe we'll find out later what it was.
It's kinda like a mystery, isn't it? Wouldn't it be fun
to pretend you're a detective trying to solve an important case? Let's see, the case of the hidden message in the newspaper. Boy, wish I were a kid again.
I'd love to see if I could figure out what she found
without being discovered," Daniel said, squinting at
the shelf and continuing to dust.

"I like a mystery, too, but it don't seem right.
You know, to spy on my own sister. But I bet I could
find out what she saw." Clay chewed on his thumb-
nail, his brow furrowed.

"This would just be a game. We would never
reveal anything that would embarrass her. Oh, I'm
sure you could find out what she saw, but remember, a great detective is like a shadow," Daniel said,
looking at the ceiling. "You know, always discovering
secrets but never being the one discovered."

"Well, if it's just a game, then it would be

okay," Clay agreed, his eyes wide with excitement. "I know I could do it. Give me a couple of days, and I'll know everything she saw in those papers."

"Yes, of course it's just a game," Daniel said. "Now, don't get yourself in trouble with your sister, or your grandmother. I wouldn't want them to ever think I gave you any bad ideas."

"Naw, you didn't give me anything. You just said "wouldn't it be fun?" The rest was my idea, wasn't it?"

"That's true," Daniel said with a smile. "But I don't want to lose my job over this."

"If I get caught—and I won't—I'll never mention your name, I promise. I'll just say I was playing a game." Clay turned back to the shelf and started wiping it down.

Sarah hollered from the kitchen doorway, "Hey! Can one of you help me with these buckets of water? I don't want to break my neck."

She groaned as she set the buckets down on the top step.

Daniel and Clay both jumped at the sound of her voice, and rushed to get the water.

"You should have called me, Miss Sarah. You don't need to be lifting heavy buckets like that," Daniel said.

Clay rolled his eyes and piped up, "She's been liftin' 'em since she was my age. Why shouldn't she?"

"Well," Daniel said patiently, "when she was your age, she was still growing, still just a young girl, but when she becomes a young woman, it's up to us men folk to recognize that, and start treating her like the lady that she's become."

"Lady," Clay spluttered. "Lady? Sarah? That's funny. That's really funny."

Sarah jerked away, stomped over to the basket of rags and dug through them.

"Clay," Daniel whispered sternly. "You catch more flies with honey than vinegar."

When he saw the puzzled look on Clay's face, he lowered his voice almost to a whisper. "You'll find out more if you're nice to her."

A knowing look came over Clay and he nodded.

"Sorry, Sarah, I was just kidding. I was just noticing that you've been looking awfully pretty lately."

"Oh, shut up, Little Clay. That first remark is just what I'd expect you to say. The second remark is a lie... you know it and I know it. Just stay away from me." Tears filled her eyes.

"Gosh, Sarah, I didn't mean to make you cry. Can't you take a joke?" Clay looked at Daniel for help, but Daniel went to Sarah, and dug through the rags with her.

"Don't mind him," Daniel said softly. "I noticed how pretty you were the first time I saw you, and I've seen some pretty women. Most of 'em had to work really hard to be attractive but on you, it just comes natural. That's the best kind. Ask any man." He found the rag he wanted and quickly looked away.

Sarah turned slowly and watched him from the corner of her eye. Her face felt flushed, and her heart beat just a little faster. It was her first compliment from a man, and she didn't know how she was supposed to react.

The rest of the morning went quickly. Daniel kept moving the water bucket around so it would be near Sarah. Even Clay did his best to help, and always hurried to her side to help her.

Eventually, she gave him a smile, and he responded with a grin. The shelves were dusted and washed. The floors turned out to be solid stone after all the dirt was removed and soon, it too, was clean, and several odd boxes were stored in various corners, out of the way.

It was late afternoon when they stood and stretched their strained backs, sore arms, and stiff necks. Sarah looked around, admiring the clean cellar.

"Gram will be surprise and pleased, I'll bet. Clay, you did a fine job. I'll be sure to tell Pa. And Daniel," Sarah smiled shyly, "it would have taken us several days to do all this without you. Thank you very much."

"Dear lady, every knight throughout the land dreams of pleasing the lady of the castle. I could do no better than to make the Princess of Eagle Creek smile." He threw out his arm, swept it across his chest, drew his left leg back, and gave a lordly bow.

Clay took up the hint and he, too, bowed deeply.

"Oh, you two. Behave." Sarah giggled and hid the smile behind her hand. "We must hurry and clean up. Supper should be ready soon, and Gram doesn't like us to be late."

Sarah snatched up the wet rags to hang up outside, while Daniel picked up the buckets. Clay grabbed the broom and homemade dust pan.

When they entered the kitchen after washing up, Mary was setting the table, while Irene dished up some potatoes.

Lillian took the last piece of sizzling, fried chicken from the enormous skillet on the stove. Her hair was pasted to her forehead from the steam escaping the skillet, and she looked pale and hollow-eyed.

"Lillian, are you feeling ill?" Sarah asked, concerned. "You don't look well."

"I didn't sleep much last night, that's all," she answered, wiping her damp brow. "The weather is so clammy and warm. Maybe I'll go outside a moment for a breath of air, if you don't mind."

She laid down the fork and shakily turned toward the door.

"I'll go with you," Sarah said in alarm.

"No, I'll be fine. I just need to rest a bit." Lillian took a deep breath and walked outside.

"Is she all right?" Clay asked, seeing the worry on his sister's face.

"She probably got a little overheated," Mary said, and patted her brother's head.

Irene smiled at their concern. "She's just overdone it today. Sometimes we work harder than our body wants us to, and our minds remind us now and then to slow down."

Clayton and Joseph walked in, drying their hands on a towel that had been by the pump. Joseph went to his wife and kissed her cheek.

"Smells wonderful, Bob, but y'all should have fixed something easier on a hot day like today. I noticed Lillian sitting outside. Did something happen?" Joseph asked.

"You're right. It is too hot to be frying chicken," she answered. "I think she went outside to catch a cool breeze. You two sit down and eat. Sarah, Mary, and I will get the food on the table. You've worked hard, too. I know you all must be starving."

"I think I'll go check on her," Clayton said.

"Wait," Irene said, almost in a whisper. "Let me go. The girls can get supper on the table."

She untied her apron, brushed her hair from her face, and stepped out the kitchen door."

"Do you think she's got pneumonia, Pa?" Clay asked, his face twisted in concern. The boy looked into his father's eyes, his bottom lip trembling. "Does she have the same sickness Ma had?"

"No, son, it's not pneumonia. She's plumb wore out. I'm sure she got overheated cooking supper. You hush your frettin', and sit down and eat."

"We're all hot, Papa, but she really looked ill," Sarah said, and stretched to catch a glimpse of Lillian through the window.

"Let the grown-ups worry about Lillian, child," Joseph admonished. "You sit down and eat."

"I'm not a child any longer," Sarah protested, glancing around shyly. "I'm almost sixteen, and wasn't Ma nearly married at sixteen?"

"No, she was nearer eighteen when she and your Pa married, and she wasn't really grown then, either," Joseph growled. "That has nothing to do with this. The girl isn't used to cooking over a hot stove like your Gram is."

"You think that's what's wrong with her?" Clay looked at the chicken leg he held.

"Never you mind," Clayton answered. "Let's get on with supper. They'll be in shortly. Now let's say the blessing."

The meal continued quietly while everyone

waited for Lillian and Irene to return. Then the door opened and Irene entered, holding the door open for Lillian. The color had returned to Lillian's face and although she was smiling, Clayton noticed her nose was pink, and her eyes looked a little swollen. They neared the table and Clayton rose, pulled out a chair, and Lillian sat down.

"Lillian, are you feeling better?" Sarah asked.

"Yes, much better. I got too warm standing over the stove so long. It's cooler outside, and I'm fine now."

"Sarah, I want you and Mary to start taking on more cooking duties from now on," Clayton said. "Your grandmother has been working too hard, and Lillian is spending too much time doing your work. Little... sorry, Clay, you'll bring in the firewood for the stove, and help your Grandma with the weeding from now on.

"Lillian has a life of her own and she shouldn't make herself sick coming out to visit, and ending up doing your work, should she?"

"No, Pa," they all mumbled, glancing around at each other.

"Lillian, I'm really sorry if we..." Sarah said softly.

"Now, don't you worry, dears. I'm fine, just fine," Lillian said, smiling as she reached over and shakily laid a hand over Sarah's.

After supper, Irene fixed tea for herself and Lillian, and coffee for the men. Clayton picked up the tray and they followed him onto the front porch. The girls, with Clay's help, cleared the table and prepared to wash the dishes.

"Lillian, Clayton's right about you doing too

much work around here. I have no doubt that you work hard at your own place, and then come out here and double up to help us," Joseph remarked, as he packed tobacco in his pipe, and tamped it down tightly.

"You all are too kind," Lillian said, her eyes filling with tears. "I can't believe that you all are so worried about someone like me, who you hardly know. However, I must admit that I feel closer to you all in the short time we've known one another, than I ever felt with anyone around here.

"There're things you don't know about me, and I feel that the way our relationship has grown, I owe it to you to be honest about certain things. First of all, Uncle William is a prince of a man. He accepts me as I am, and has never judged me, nor has he disclosed what happened to me this past year.

"I wanted to go east and ride this out, but he wouldn't have it. He insisted I stay with him, and jokingly said if I tried to leave, he'd follow me to the ends of the earth to take care of me. He would, too.

"If anyone in town knew what I've been through, they would all be hovering and patronizing and, of course, judging me. I simply couldn't stand that. I didn't want anyone to know."

"Know?" Joseph said, leaning forward. "Know what, for heaven's sake?

Lillian hitched a sob, took a deep breath, and sighed. "Six months ago, I took a trip to Charlotte to visit Aunt Ester, who I am particularly fond of," Lillian began her story. "Her best friend, Margaret, lived next door to her with her daughter, Edna Applegate, and Edna's son, David.

"Edna's late husband and his family had been

members of Charlottes' elite high society. Although
Margaret could have cared less about that sort of
thing, Edna reveled in being one of the crème de la
crème. Edna was planning to take David to Europe in
hopes of matching him with someone with a title,
and hopefully, royal blood. I'm telling you all this so
you'll understand why we did what we did."

Lillian paused and stared out into the darkness.

"Go ahead, dear, you're among friends,"
Irene coaxed with a soft, gentle tone.

"After a few weeks, David and I fell in love,"
Lillian said softly. "His mother forbid him to see me,
and sped up her plans to leave for Europe immediately. And to make a long story a little shorter, we
eloped and got married."

Clayton cleared his throat, and shot a quick
glance at Joseph, who was still leaning forward in his
chair.

"Go on, Lillian," Irene encouraged.

"We sent his mother, and my aunt, a telegram
announcing our marriage. David went to the local
bank to make arrangements to have his money transferred to Rock Hill, and discovered that his mother
had frozen his account. Apparently she, too, was on
the account, and made sure we had no money. We
were able to pay our hotel bill, and caught a stage
back to Charlotte that very day.

"We went directly to Margaret's house but
Edna refused to allow me in. I took my things and
went to Aunt Ester, who welcomed me with open
arms. I could tell she was caught between her
friendship with Margaret, and her feelings for me. I
was, after all, family.

"David and I saw each other on the sly every

chance we got, and behind Edna's back, of course. She was in the process of having our marriage annulled. David insisted he could change her mind, but he never got the chance. About two months ago, just a few weeks before you arrived, we made plans to meet in a hotel restaurant in downtown Charlotte.

"We spent several hours planning our future, although one that was not to be. We left the hotel together, and he hailed a buggy. He was going to get out at the corner and walk to his house, while the carriage would take me to my door..."

Lillian paused and sucked in a shaky breath, while tears spilled down her cheeks. Joseph reached into his vest pocket and handed her his handkerchief. She wiped her eyes and gave him a grateful smile.

"We never made it to the corner. The driver of an oncoming carriage lost control of his horses when a windblown paper spooked them. His carriage careened into ours, forcing us up onto the sidewalk, where we overturned. I woke up in the hospital with Aunt Ester by my side. When I asked about David, she began to cry and I knew—I just knew."

Lillian took a deep breath.

"Edna accused me of causing her son's death. She needn't have bothered. I blamed myself, too. Because I had broken my collarbone and my arm, I never got to see him again, nor was I allowed to attend the funeral. David had our marriage license, and apparently Edna destroyed it. She never acknowledged our marriage, or that I ever existed. As soon as the doctor told me I could travel, I came home, and here I am." She smiled wryly, although her eyes still glistened with tears.

Clayton listened to Lillian's story, and as it

progressed, his eyes narrowed. He sat silently when she finished, and stared blankly at the wooden porch floor.

"Bob, did you know about this?" Joseph asked his wife, who had put her arm around Lillian's trembling shoulders.

"She told me a little when I went to see about her at suppertime. But I didn't know any details."

Lillian drew herself up straight in the chair. She held her head high, smiled, and took a sip of her tea.

"No one knows about this but Uncle William, and now, you all. Although Uncle William has been nothing but kind and loving, I simply can't burden him with the result of my actions."

"But my dear," Irene murmured softly, "you know he'll understand. No doubt he'll welcome the addition to the family."

"Addition," Joseph said quizzically. "Addition? What in the world are you talkin'... oh, my word... addition!" His face reddened when realization of her meaning hit him.

"No, I couldn't do this to him. But you are right. He would understand, and he would pretend to be absolutely thrilled, but you don't understand. It's not his attitude I'm worried about. It's what he would have to endure because of me.

"Sycamore Grove has had its share of secrets surface from time to time but the doctor, the minister, sheriff, and banker, are members of this community who people confide in, and trust. They have heard confessions and indiscretions, treated private, embarrassing medical problems, are aware of young, foolish unlawful pranks, and have pertinent information about the financial situations of many upstanding leaders.

"Believe me when I say the town's people wouldn't be comfortable if they knew their most dreaded transgressions were known by someone involved in a scandal. I couldn't put my uncle in that position."

"When did you know?" Clayton asked, his voice almost a whisper.

"I haven't felt well for a couple of weeks but tonight it dawned on me, and when Irene came out to check on me... she..."

Lillian broke down in tears. She kept her head down, not able to look him in the eye. She quickly wiped her eyes on her sleeve.

"It's foolish not to pay attention to yourself, I know, but it's been so hard trying to pretend that nothing happened, that I didn't fall in love, marry, and become a widow within a few weeks.

"Ladies don't do that sort of thing. Ladies accept propriety, acknowledge laws of respectability, and I have had to ignore my emotions, and be the happy-go-lucky, head-strong woman that causes the town to shake their heads at my daring. I... I never allowed myself to think... I never imagined that I, I..." Lillian stopped mid-sentence, and tears once again cascaded down her cheeks.

"None of that matters now," Irene said. Her right eyebrow shot up while she glared at Clayton, and her look dared Joseph to open his mouth.

Both men had seen that look before and knew better than defy Irene's mood.

"No, of course not, everything'll work out," Clayton said, clearing his throat.

He, like Joseph, leaned forward but Clayton seemed to be a million miles away, as he unconsciously twisted his wedding ring. He stood and when he did, there was a clinking sound as the ring fell to the floor. He stared at it for several seconds before picking it up.

"I have to go." Lillian's voice was weak, and she was trembling.

"Have another cup of tea, dear," Irene said gently.

"No, thank you. I feel totally drained, and I just need to lie down."

"I'll get your horse." Daniel spoke for the first time since they sat on the porch.

"No, she mustn't ride her horse home. She's too upset, and it isn't good in her condition," Clayton snapped. "Help me hitch up the wagon and I'll drive her home. We'll tie her horse to the back."

"Please, don't go to any trouble. I'll be fine," Lillian begged.

"It's no trouble, Lillian. We both need some fresh air. I'll be right back."

In a short time, Clayton pulled the wagon up front with Lillian's horse tied to the back. Joseph and Daniel helped Lillian into the wagon, and stood silently watching.

Irene waved, and Clayton popped the reins starting the horses forward. Lillian gave a weak smile toward the family who had befriended her, then turned as the wagon made the circle to the road.

As Clayton and Lillian disappeared toward town, Daniel slipped away and headed toward his room in the barn, while Joseph and Irene returned to the kitchen.

~ * ~

For the first few, very long minutes, neither

Clayton nor Lillian spoke. Lillian gave a slight jump when Clayton broke the silence.

"My mother died before I was old enough to remember her, and my father, like Daniel's, was a gambler. He dragged me all over the country, searching for that *lucky game* where he planned to make his fortune.

He was killed when they caught him cheating, and I was only five years old. Being raised in an orphanage, and with Susan being an only child, we always wanted a large family of six or seven. Having a family meant a lot to her and me. Little Clay just turned three when she died."

"I'm so sorry. Irene told me about Susan, and what a wonderful wife and mother she was. If she was anything like her mother, she was an angel. Losing her had to be devastating for you and the children."

Clayton flinched, his face reflecting the emotion of loss, of fleeting pain. "It was. If I had been alone, I'm not sure what would have happened to me. But I had the children to be strong for, and with Joseph and Irene supporting me, I was able to survive. Susan made me a better man. I wanted to be everything for her, and now, I want to be everything for my children."

"That's an admirable goal. I can see by the shine in their eyes when they look at you, they love you, and are proud of you. I have no doubt that you'll continue to be their hero."

"Don't know much 'bout being a hero," Clayton mumbled, staring at the knotted reins in his clenched fist. "But I do know about working hard, and wanting the best for my family. Nothing in this life is free, not even that house back there. I may not have paid near what this place is worth, but I do know that I will work hard to earn the privilege of living there. We've been given a second chance in life, and for that blessing, we'll be forever grateful."

"No one deserves it more than you all do, Clayton."

"Thank you."

Clayton was surprised to see the lights of town appear so much sooner than he expected. He felt they hadn't left the house more than ten minutes ago, and now they were almost at Lillian's front door.

He pulled the team near the front gate, tied the reins around the brake handle, and jumped to the ground. He hurried around to the other side, and reached for Lillian the moment she threw her leg to the wheel, and caught her as her boot slipped from the sandy rim.

"You gotta be careful now, Lillian," Clayton said, a catch in his throat. "That could have been a nasty fall."

"I will, Clayton. Thank you."

Clayton walked around to untie Lillian's horse. Taking the reins, he led the horse to the stable, removed the saddle, and left him in the stall. Clayton went back to his wagon, jerked off his hat, and watched Lillian open the gate. She paused, looked back, and with a tight smile, slowly walked across the gravel to the porch. Lillian looked back one more time, smiled again, and disappeared inside the house.

Clayton reached into his pocket and fingered the wedding band that had slipped off his finger earlier that evening. He smiled wryly and glanced up at the stars.

"Dagnabbit, Susan, are you positive this is what I must do?"

He stared at the sky and noticed a shooting star flare across the heavens. Clayton shook his head in wonder while he mounted the wagon, and clucked at the horses. Heading back to Eagle Creek, he dreaded the conversation he was about to have with his family, but have it he would—after all, it did concern the entire family.

~ * ~

Daniel heard the wagon wheels crunch up the graveled driveway and stop just outside the barn door. He jumped up and met Clayton, who was pushing the double doors open. Daniel grabbed the halter of the nearest horse, and led the team into the confines of the building. When the young man began to unhitch the wagon, Clayton nodded his thanks. Daniel noticed Clayton's tight-lipped expression as he led the horses into the stalls, fastened the door, and pitched a little hay to them.

"Good night, Daniel, and thanks." Clayton nodded again.

"No problem," Daniel said.

~ * ~

Clayton took a deep breath when he saw Irene and Joseph sitting in the kitchen having coffee. He was glad they hadn't gone to their room, at least he didn't have to get them out of bed for this discussion.

"Well, how is she?" Joseph asked, setting his cup on the table.

"She's fine, I guess... considering." Clayton frowned, took his hat off, and jammed it on the rack.

"Poor little thing," Irene said, shaking her head. "A situation like this should be a happy time, a time to share with your husband, and to announce to your mother that she's going to be a grandma. That child has neither, and I truly worry about her."

"Well, it's her situation I want to talk to you about," Clayton said.

He shifted his weight uncomfortably from one foot to the other. He cleared his throat and rubbed his forehead. Clayton watched Joseph poured some coffee from his cup into his saucer and blow on the steaming liquid before taking a noisy slurp.

"I can't believe that young man's mother was such a monster. Any family should be proud to have Lillian as part of their family. She's lovely, kind, generous, and not afraid of hard work. She'll make someone a fine wife, and she'll be a good mother, too," Joseph said.

Clayton nodded. "Yes, that's exactly what I think, and I'm glad you feel that way. Irene, would you mind asking the children to join us? What I'm about to say concerns us all."

Irene raised a brow and pursed her lips but went to get her grandchildren. She paused at the foot of the staircase and raised her voice slightly.

"Sarah. Mary. Clay. Come down here, please. Your father wants to talk to us."

Mary's was the first to appear at the rail, looking down at her grandmother.

"What's wrong?"

"Nothing I know of, honey. Just get your sister and little brother, and come to the kitchen."

"Okay, Gram. We'll be there in a minute."

Irene went back to the kitchen and sat down heavily. Placing her elbows on the table, she leaned

Bobbie Shafer

forward and rubbed the back of her neck.

"Bob, don't tell me you're coming down with something," Joseph said. He looked at his wife, concern etched across his face.

"No, no, I'm not sick. It's just that besides being tired, I feel so bad about Lillian."

The children appeared at the door. Mary and Sarah in their gowns and robes, and Clay Jr. in his pajamas, his robe slung over one shoulder. He yawned and peered through sleep-swollen eyes at his dad.

"What is it, Pa? Did we do something wrong?"

"No, son, none of you did anything wrong. I want to ask your opinion about doing something right. Something I feel is right, that is, but I want to know honestly how you all feel about it."

"What is it, Pa?" Mary asked

"Well, as you know, Lillian has been a great friend to us since the very first day we arrived here," Clayton continued.

"She sure has. She never forgets to bring us candy," Clay said, his eyes glowing with the thought.

"Hush, Clay. Listen to Papa," Sarah said, and touched her little brother's shoulder.

"Sorry," the boy said.

Joseph and Irene looked at one another, and then back to Clayton.

Suddenly, Clayton's tongue felt glued to the roof of his mouth. His mind grew cloudy. The right words seemed stuck in his throat, and he felt numb.

"Son, spit it out. What's on your mind? We're more than a family, we're of one mind around here. If you've got a problem, then we've all got a problem. Lay it out on the table, Clayton, and we'll get it fixed," Joseph said.

"Sit down, honey, relax," Irene said softly, and motioned toward a chair.

"I've been thinking about asking Lillian to marry me," Clayton blurted out on a rush of air, and then sat heavily in the nearest chair.

The statement was received in total silence.

"Marry Lillian, Pa? I've never seen you say more than a few words to her. I can't believe you two are that close," Sarah finally said, after opening and closing her mouth several times.

"Would she be our ma?" Clay asked, and struggled into the robe that kept slipping off his shoulders.

Mary and Sarah looked from their brother to their father, waiting for his response.

Before he could answer, Irene rose, went to her grandson and put her hands on his shoulders.

"Your mother will always be your mother. Nothing and no one can ever replace her. But life sometimes offers alternatives. In this case, Lillian could be your friend, a companion, someone you could talk to, get advice from, and you would learn to love her," Irene said, and hugged her grandson.

"Are you saying you think this is a good idea?" Joseph asked, folding his arms on the table, and resting his chin on his hands.

"What I'm saying is that if this is what Clayton wants to do—what he thinks is best—then I feel we should support him."

Joseph looked at his wife, and then at Clayton. He leaned back and slowly nodded.

"Do you love her, Pa?" Mary looked at her father, her face open and innocent.

"Lillian is a fine woman, and I think she will be a good wife, and fit into this family. It will be good to have a grown up woman to help your Gran, and I know she will enjoy Lillian's company."

"But Mary asked if you love her," Sarah said, the words clipped.

"Not like I loved your mother, not like I love you, and not like I love your Papa Joe and Gran. But I'm very fond of Lillian, and I think that's a good start."

Clay Jr. yawned and blinked. "Okay, Pa, if that's what you want."

"I just don't understand your rush," Sarah said. "You don't know anything about her. Why don't you give it some time, court her, take her for long drives, and get to know her. Why ask her now?"

Joseph stared at his granddaughter, and then turned to see Clayton's reaction.

Again Clayton cleared his throat. "Life's too short, Sarah. Time often slips away before you realize it. I know all I need to about her, and I feel this is the right thing to do. Still, I want this decision to be one that has been approved by each and every one of you. If any one of you disapproves of Lillian joining our family, then we'll pretend that this conversation never took place, and we'll go on living our lives just like we always have. "

"It's your decision, Pa. You've always taught us to make decisions with our minds as well as our hearts, and if you think this is the right thing to do, then so do we." Mary reached over and touched Sarah's arm.

Sarah took a deep breath and squared her shoulders. "Mary's right, Pa, we'll support you. Go ahead, ask her. I like Lillian. She's a nice person. She'll fit in here, we'll see to that."

"Joseph, how do you feel about this?"

Clayton cocked his head, and waited. He knew Joseph was all about family. He had reluctantly welcomed Clayton into his family many years ago, and learned to love him as if he were his own son. Still this was pushing a little hard.

Now he was asking Joseph to accept a woman he barely knew to become a member of the family, and to hold a position that had been filled by the daughter he had loved more than life itself. It all came down to Joseph. Although he had a good heart, this was asking a lot—was it too much?

He saw Joseph grab his cup and hold it out toward Irene. Clayton felt his mother-in-law pat his shoulder, as she went to get the coffee pot. He watched her fill her husband's cup, and slip into her chair.

Joseph slowly raised his cup, blew on the steaming contents and took a sip. He sat the cup on the table, and looked back at Clayton.

"When you were just a misguided lad, who appeared out of nowhere to court my sweet, innocent Susan, I was skeptical. However, I was also impressed by your patience and determination to win my approval.

"Nevertheless, I must admit that at the time, I did not think you were good enough for her. I didn't think anyone was good enough for her. Eventually, I could see that you understood the bond between Susan and her mother and I, and I knew you would do nothing to cause Susan distress.

"I could also see that you loved her enough that you would walk away rather than cause her pain. That was the factor that turned the tide. You were meant to be a part of our family."

Joseph's voice always became shaky whenever he spoke of his daughter. "In all these years, you have never failed to make me proud of you. I can't say I agreed with all your decisions, but in the end, I could see they were meant to benefit the children, and I would have been wrong to interfere." His voice trembled with emotion. Joseph paused, pulled out his wadded up handkerchief, and loudly blew his nose.

"Again we are faced with an idea that is difficult, and again, I'm not sure I understand your reasoning. However, saying that, I must agree with the others. We are all fond of Lillian, and considering the situation, we will welcome her to Eagle Creek and our family.

"Did you talk to her when you took her home? What does she think?"

Clayton allowed himself a slight smile. He rose and paced back and forth.

"Thank you all. I know I have sprung this on you without any warning, and you have made this easier than I thought possible.

"To answer your question, Joseph, no, I have not brought the subject up to Lillian. I thought I should discuss this with y'all first. I didn't want to make this decision alone. I will go to her house first thing in the morning. I don't want to waste any time."

"I still don't understand the rush," Sarah said, a frown marring her pretty face.

Irene rose and slipped her arm around her granddaughter's shoulders. "You will soon, dear. I promise you."

She looked at Clayton, who nodded.

"Mary, take your brother back upstairs and get him into bed. He's about to fall asleep."

"Yes, Gram. Are you coming, Sarah?"

"Sarah's going to help me clean up and wash the cups. We'll get the coffee pot ready for in the morning."

"Goodnight," Mary said, tugging on Clay, and led him, stumbling, down the hall.

"Joseph, why don't you and Clayton go on to bed? Sarah and I will finish up here, and I'll be in shortly." Irene emphasized her remark by motioning toward the door.

"But I haven't finished my coffee," Joseph complained, apparently missing the plan.

"Yes, you have. If you drink anymore, you won't get any sleep. Go on, now, Sarah and I need to get through."

"Okay, okay. You don't need to be so bossy," Joseph growled, scooting his chair back, and looking at Clayton. "I can tell we're not wanted around here. Guess we'd better turn in. See ya in the morning, Son." Joseph patted Clayton on the arm.

"Good night, Papa Joe," Clayton said.

When the men were gone, Irene filled Sarah in on Lillian's dilemma, with the promise that what she was told would remain confidential. She explained how distraught Lillian was, not for herself but how having the baby would cause her uncle to be the center of local gossip, and possibly destroy his reputation.

"I don't understand how Lillian having a child would hurt her uncle's position," Sarah said, shaking her head.

"Even though Lillian is old enough to make her own decisions," Irene said, "some people would blame him for not having better control over his niece. Some people would say he should have raised her better, or made sure she was taught better.

"Those gossipy crones could, and probably would, start rumors that could destroy his good name, and the name of his family. Lillian has examined the situation and, to be honest, the thought that she might try to take off and bear this burden alone, has crossed my mind. Apparently your father came to the same conclusion."

"I never thought of Pa in the same way I thought of a knight in shining armor, but he is definitely brave," Sarah said.

"Well, I don't know if this is quite that dramatic." Irene smiled at her granddaughter's remark. "But I'll have to admit, this is quite a sacrifice for a man like him to make."

"What do you mean a man like him?"

"Your father pulled himself up by his own boot straps. He never had the love and upbringing of caring parents. When he met your mother, he learned what caring, devotion, faith, and belonging to a family truly meant. He became a dedicated and committed husband, and then a father. His entire world rotated around his wife, his children, and I'm proud to say, your grandfather and me.

"Your father's decision to marry Lillian will mean more work, more responsibility, and definitely more stress and worry. Your papa is a good man, even better than I gave him credit for. I'm proud of him. I hope you are, too."

"Oh, Gram, I never thought of it like that. I guess I was just jealous. It's only been Mary, Little Clay, me and Pa for so long. But I see now that he's marrying Lillian to help her, not because we're not important anymore."

"Sarah, of course y'all are important. You see, your Pa could care less about what people think. He's a loving man who will stand by you, your sister and brother, no matter what you do, or what problems you might have to face. He just couldn't allow Lillian to suffer because of narrow-minded, judgmental, hypocrites who think they are better than others.

"Go to bed now and remember—Lillian's secret is our secret. I'm depending on you not to repeat what I told you to anyone, not to Mary, or Little Clay, and not Daniel. They will know in time, when your Pa or Lillian decides to share."

"I swear, Gram," Sarah vowed solemnly. She kissed her grandmother on the cheek and hurried upstairs.

~NINE~
The Family Grows

The next morning, Clayton took an extensive bath and dressed with care, smoothing each wrinkle, and reinforcing every crease. After combing his hair, he applied a tiny bit of hair oil that he had bought for special occasions, and this was as special as an occasion could get. He stepped back and surveyed his reflection, and sighed.

The grimace on the face that looked back was that of a man who was about to have an ingrown toenail cut out without anesthetic. Drawing himself up straight, he practiced facial expressions. He smiled, relaxed his face, and smiled again. Shaking his head, he put on a serious expression, and tried again. This time, he smiled slightly. *That will work,* he thought.

He had practiced his speech until the wee hours of the morning, and still wasn't sure exactly what he was going to say. He would just have to play it by ear.

"Come on, sleepyheads, breakfast is ready."

Irene's cheery voice rang throughout the house, and the aroma of frying bacon tugged on everyone's senses.

The sound of feet pattering toward the kitchen made Clayton smile. Leaving his room, he started down the steps just in time to see his young son swing around the banister at the base of the staircase and dash toward the kitchen.

Pausing on the landing, Clayton took a deep breath. Looking around, he couldn't help but admire the beauty of his new house. A sense of pride en-

gulfed him when he realized that his family was all
together, everyone had settled in, and they had acquired a young man to help both in the house and
outside, plus, the fields were ready to plant. Everyone seemed comfortable, and had accepted their
new life. Hard work was ahead, but hard times
seemed only a faint memory.

Was marrying Lillian going to change all this?
Did he have to right to disrupt his family by thrusting
a practical stranger on them? Why did he feel it was
up to him to keep Lillian and her uncle out of the
circle of gossip? Starting down the last flight of
stairs, he hesitated at the bottom step and gazed
lovingly at the delicate, hand-painted, oil lamp sitting on the table.

He remembered how Sarah had held that lamp
in her lap, cradling it tenderly, and protecting it
fiercely, on the ride to Eagle Creek. The sun rose
higher in the morning sky causing a flowing beam to
reach the window on the landing, and bathed the
lamp in golden light. It seemed to shimmer before
his eyes. A peace settled over him.

"Is that you, Susan?" Clayton asked in a
hushed whisper, his eyes misting. "I need your wis-
dom. I need your strength."

The shimmering lamp trembled, and the fragile crystals seemed to sway ever so slightly.

Clayton reached for the lamp and ran his
coarse, weathered fingers tenderly over the hand-
blown globe that framed the clear-glass chimney. He
could feel no tremor but the lamp seemed to warm
under his touch.

"Oh, Susan," he sighed. "Pleasing you was always my greatest joy. I feel your presence everywhere, but am I reading the signs correctly, or is the

hole in my heart causing me to hallucinate, and imagine, that you are communicating with me?"

"Pa, who are you talking to?" Little Clay stood in the doorway, his head tilted slightly, as he glanced around the empty hall.

"Guess old age is creeping up on me, Son," Clayton said with a slight grin. He headed toward the kitchen and tousled his son's hair on the way.

"Whatcha all dressed up for, Pa?" Clay Jr. grabbed his dad's hand, and they walked to the table together.

"Good gracious, Clay," Mary said with a wry grin. "You must have been sleepwalking last night, and we just thought you were awake."

"Last night?" Little Clay's brow rose, and he waited for someone to explain.

"Don't you remember?" Mary asked, exasperated.

"Remember what? Mary, quit playing games with me. Why are y'all looking at me so funny?"

"He was tired and probably half-asleep," Irene said gently. "Your father is going to ask Lillian to marry him, and to come live here with us."

"Oh yeah, I remember that," the boy said, his face turning red. "What does that have to do with Pa getting so dressed up?"

Mary burst out laughing, and Sarah sputtered, her mouthful of oatmeal splattering across the table.

"Asking a lady for her hand in marriage is a special, dress-up time," Irene explained, trying to keep her smile to a minimum. She tossed a wet cloth to Sarah to wipe the table with.

"Like going to church, I guess," her grandson said.

"Yes, dear, like going to church."

Daniel entered the kitchen, smoothing down his damp hair, drying his hands on his pants leg.

"Morning y'all," he said with a big grin. "It sure is gonna be a fine day."

"Gosh, Daniel, isn't it kinda early to be in such a good mood?" Little Clay asked. He reached for a hot biscuit, which he tossed from hand to hand before dropping it on his plate.

"Well, today is the day my trial period as handyman is over, and since nobody knocked on the door this morning to tell me to hit the road, I figure I still got a job. That's the best reason I know to be in a good mood.

"I gotta tell you folks that working here is like being a part of a family, and you folks are the closest thing to a family that I've ever had. Getting this job was truly a blessing."

Clayton smiled. "Thank you, Daniel, I appreciate that. Your being here at this time is a blessing for us, too. We'll need you now, more than ever. I guess your trial period is truly over.

"I can pay you thirty-five cents a day for six days a week, plus room and board. There is a small cabin back a piece from the house that we can fix up for you. It might have been the original house that was on this land. There is a small sitting room, a kitchen and a bedroom. The kitchen has a woodstove and I'm sure we can find furnishings for it in the attic. Your meals will continue to be provided. I hope you'll accept these terms until I can afford to pay you more?" He looked at Daniel for a reaction.

"Yes, of course, sir. That's just great," Daniel said, reaching out to shake Clayton's hand.

"Maybe we can work on that cabin when I get back from town."

"Yes sir."

"Well, since I'm being paid now," Daniel said with a grin, "I gotta eat faster and get to work. Mister Joe can tell me what needs to be done. Thanks again. I'll see you when you get back from wherever you're going in them dress-up clothes."

He smiled and reached over to shake Clayton's hand once more.

Breakfast was rather rushed. Joseph, anxious to get the fence completed, finished his coffee, stood, and jerked his napkin from his collar. Sarah couldn't wait to find a secret corner to read Aimee's journal. Clay wanted to see if Honey remembered the tricks he taught her, and Mary just wanted to get away from everyone.

Getting attention as a middle child was hard enough, but now there would be a complete stranger being fawned over and entertained, and it just wasn't fair.

~ * ~

Daniel stared across the field, his mind racing from one thought to another. He held the wire on the fence post taut while Joseph hammered the barbed wire to the far post. Watching the older man pause and wipe the sweat from his forehead, Daniel felt admiration for the hard work this family faced day after day.

They had no regrets, no irritation, and felt blessed that life was so good. This world was strange to him. All his life he'd watched his father and grandfather scheme, plan, blame others for their failures, and then flourish in the glory of cheating someone out of their hard earned savings. It wasn't that he accepted their lifestyle as the right way to live, it was just the only way he ever knew.

Now, his thoughts reigned in confusion. Nothing was right. His entire plan was going up in smoke. Daniel had meant what he said about feeling at home here. This family did make him feel like he belonged, but he knew didn't, and never would. He was going to get to work, explore the grounds, search the house, find the gold, and disappear. Still...

He never thought he would become so involved with these people. That wasn't part of his strategy. But here he was, admiring a man who had shaken off a terrible childhood, flirting with a young girl whose face remained in his thoughts long after she left, caring for a boy who had no idea he was being used for Daniel's scheme and liking, and the older couple who treated him like family. He beat his fist against the edge of the post. It wasn't fair, it just wasn't fair.

~ * ~

Clayton let his horse, Shine, have his head as they walked toward town at an easy pace—not hurrying but not dawdling. Clayton felt guilty at leaving his family working while he went into town to add another responsibility to the household.

He almost reined Shine to a halt when he looked up. They had reached the first house at the edge of town, and William and Lillian's home was located nearby, on Hill Street. It was a large white house that seemed to be looking down on the town, but after meeting William and Lillian, he knew the Gaines family was not that type of people.

Before he could change his mind, the horse continued on his own. Turning his head slightly toward Hill Street, Shine veered up the incline, following the buggy trail without urging, and carried Clayton to the very gate where he had deposited Lillian the night before. Clayton sat frozen in his saddle, staring at the horse's head bobbing up and down, seeming secretly pleased with himself at arriving at the correct destination without much direction.

"Mercy, Susan, you are the most determined woman I've ever known," Clayton said, glancing at the cloudless sky, his heart pounding in his chest.

He dismounted, the front door opened and Lillian walked onto the small porch, pulling her hair back and twisting it up. Securing the soft, honey-colored curls, she watched Clayton reach over, un-latch the gate and pull his hat off as he entered.

She started to smile and then her demeanor changed. "Clayton, what brings you into town so early? Is anyone sick? Is something wrong? You look strange."

"Everyone's fine, Lillian, and nothing's wrong. If I look strange, it's because I need to talk to you, and I'm worried that I won't find the right words."

"Clayton, you know how fond I've become of you, and your family. Whatever you need of me, all you have to do is ask. Why don't you come in and have some coffee? Uncle William is at the bank. Agnes, the housekeeper, is shopping, and we'll have some time to ourselves before she returns."

"Are you sure William won't object to me being here without a chaperone?"

Lillian threw back her head. Her laughter sounded like bells to Clayton. She reached out, took his arm, and pulled him toward the front door.

"Clayton, William isn't that old fashioned. It isn't like I'm inviting a complete stranger to share coffee with me. That would be foolish, and he knows that I've had enough foolishness in my past not to repeat it."

With a nervous grin, Clayton allowed Lillian to slip her arm under his, and lead him through the door into the kitchen.

Clayton sat still and stiff in the chair, his mind nervously fingering the words he wanted to say. His eyes darted around the room taking in every detail, while Lillian poured coffee into cups on the counter. The room was spotless, cheery, and more than comfortable. It was inviting.

"Your housekeeper does a great job of cleaning," Clayton said, trying to fill the silence between them.

"Yes, she is very efficient. She sweeps, dusts, washes, and keeps the beds in fresh linens, but the kitchen is my domain. I love my kitchen. I'm afraid sitting in the parlor, being waited on hand and foot is just not my cup of tea. Cooking, polishing, washing the windows, and tending to the herb garden makes my heart sing. Don't ask me why, it just does."

"We all have things in our lives that fulfill us. For me, other than spending time with my family, is working with the earth and, like you, I can't tell you why. I wasn't raised to be a farmer, and I've spent most of my working life at the mill, but when the sweet-smelling earth rolls open beneath the blades of the plow to accept the seeds that will produce food for my family, and grain for the animals, it gives me great joy."

Lillian smiled and placed Clayton's cup on the table. She slid into the chair opposite him and cocked her head to the side, smiling.

"Now, what is so important that you took time

from your family and that sweet-smelling soil to talk to me?"

Clayton's mind was steady but his hand trembled slightly, causing the coffee to come dangerously close to spilling. He lifted his cup to his lips, and after a long sip, he replaced the cup in the saucer, took a deep breath, exhaled and leaned forward.

"I have a proposition for you, Lillian. One that I feel will be beneficial to both of us. My children are my life, and their grandparents have been more than generous in helping me raise them. I am so grateful to have them in my life. Still, a man needs a companion, a partner, a woman who will share in the decisions, laugh with the joys, and comfort the tears. I am no different.

"You are a fine woman, who is also in need of a family, partner, and companion. You need someone to share your burdens, your decisions, your laughter, and your tears. I think we would be good for one another. I would be honored if you would consent to be my wife, partner, and companion.

"I realize that my offer includes the responsibility of a ready-made family, the hard work of farm life, but I promise to be there for you, stand by you, consider your feelings, and protect you with my life.

"Lillian, will you marry me?"

Lillian listened quietly and when Clayton spoke his final words, she sat, cup suspended halfway between the table and her mouth.

Fortunately there was just a drop of coffee left in her cup. When she replied, she waved her cup back and forth as if she were conducting an orchestra.

"Marry you? Clayton, have you lost your mind? There's a baby on the way—the child of another man. I don't want my mistake to interfere with the lives of you and your family."

Clayton reached over and picked up Lillian's free hand. She sat the cup down.

"I don't believe that life occurs by accident, or that the love of a baby could do anything but bring joy to anyone's life. Marry me, Lillian, and be a part of my world. You won't regret it, I promise you."

"Your marriage to Susan was built on love, as was my marriage to David. What about love, Clayton? Have you given up on love?"

Clayton watched Lillian's eyes fill with tears, and then spill over, and trickle down her cheeks. He rose, went to Lillian, and knelt by her side.

"Your heart is filled with love, Lillian. Love for your late husband, your baby, your uncle, and your town. Susan filled my heart with love. That love, in turn, encompasses my children, my in-laws, and allowes me the joy of life. Love can't be denied, Lillian, and I think, in time, we might discover that love for one another."

"What if we don't, Clayton? What if, in time, as you put it, we realize we feel nothing for each other?"

"I don't believe in nothing, Lillian, and I don't think you do either. We'll be too busy living, teaching, sharing, and loving our children to feel nothing.

"There won't be any demand that can't be met. This union, for now, will be for today, for the children, those now and those to come, and we'll let tomorrow's worry wait until tomorrow. No sense in worrying about the unknown when there's so much we can see needs done today. Don't you agree?"

Lillian mulled Clayton's words over carefully. She looked into his eyes, and saw the shine and clarity of sincerity. She had been on the verge of sinking into the despair of depression, and although she had fought it with her every breath, she hadn't been sure she'd win. As it was, her foolish actions were sure to bring shame on her uncle, ridicule on her child, and wagging tongues about her life.

She had no proof of her marriage to David, and no one, not one single soul, would believe she had been married. She wasn't even sure William would have believed her if Aunt Edna hadn't been there to inform him about what had happened.

Clayton's proposal had been a complete surprise, and she wasn't sure what had prompted it, although she was sure it was just from the goodness of his heart.

Although her first impulse was to loudly protest the proposal and refuse, her second thought was more rational, more sensible. It was the perfect solution to the problems her pregnancy would create. It was the answer to prevent any future problems that she would have to face otherwise. She could help Clayton with the children, his mother-in-law with the household work, and be a good companion to him. It might work. It could work. It had to work.

"Thank you, Clayton," Lillian finally said. "I will marry you. My heart tells me what a sacrifice you are making, and my mind tells me I can't refuse. Yes, I will be your wife, and I will be forever grateful for your kindness."

"It is I who is grateful, Lillian. This is the right thing to do. You won't be sorry. I'll make you a good husband."

"I know you will, Clayton. I know you will."

Clayton took her hand and kissed it tenderly. Taking his hat, he turned and walked to the door.

"I'm going to the bank to tell your uncle, Lillian. Let's hope he takes it well. I'm not sure how he'll react."

"Wait. I'm going with you. I think it'll be easier with me by your side. I know he'll be shocked about the proposal considering the surprise element, but he'll probably be secretly pleased that I'll be someone else's responsibility.

"Hopefully, he'll think we've been seeing each other in secret. Still, for his sake, and yours, if I'm with you, maybe he won't wonder why this is coming out of the blue."

"I guess I should have asked him first," Clayton said, frowning.

"Times are changing, Clayton. Uncle William knows that."

"I'll go hitch up the buggy if you're going with me," Clayton said and headed for the stable.

~ * ~

William Gaines opened the bank door, and Mrs. Elvira MacKenzie shuffled slowly onto the sidewalk, leaning heavily on a highly polished ebony cane.

"Don't you worry Miss Elvira, I'll guard that ten dollar deposit of yours with my life," he assured her.

"You'd better, you young whippersnapper. I wouldn't trust someone as young as you if I hadn't knowed yer daddy. I 'spect he raised you right," the woman said, and gave William a scathing stare.

William smiled patiently as Elvira waddled toward the general store. He looked up and noticed Clayton Wilkins, along with his niece, in a wagon heading toward the bank. William waited until Clayton tied up the horses, then assisted Lillian from the wagon, and held the door open for them.

"Uncle William, do you have time to talk to us for a few minutes?" Lillian asked, and glanced at Clayton, who rotated his hat in his hands nervously.

"As a matter of fact, I do. Come on back to my office," her uncle answered, wondering why the two of them seemed so serious.

In the office, Lillian and Clayton took the chairs in front of the desk, and William sat in his.

Neither spoke for a moment.

"You wanted to talk?" William finally broke the silence.

"Mister—uh, pardon me, William, I want to ask for your niece's hand, no that's not right, I've already asked..." Clayton's face flushed, and his tongue sounded thick.

"Uncle, Clayton has asked me to marry him, I've said yes, and we want your blessing," Lillian said, rescuing Clayton.

"Well," William said softly, "I guess I should have known that someday I'd have to face this, but I must say, this is somewhat of a surprise. However, if I have to lose you, I'm glad it's to someone as fine, trustworthy, and dependable as Clayton Wilkins.

"I guess you realize that your lifestyle and Clayton's is quite different, don't you, honey?" He looked at Lillian.

"Yes sir, I do, and I must say it's a lifestyle I feel I can easily adapt to," Lillian said, and looked fondly at Clayton.

"Clayton, you and Lillian have a lot to learn about one another. I don't know if the two of you have spent enough time together to discuss all the important factors of your pasts," William said.

"William, Lillian and I do have a lot to learn about each other, but we have a lot of time ahead to hash out all the little things. For the moment, we know the most important things. Life can sometimes be unfair, cruel, and sad, but with help from someone who understands, we can always make it through. We understand each other, and we'll make it, you can count on that." Clayton's color was back, he sat straight, and spoke with conviction.

"Then let me offer you my blessings, my prayers for happiness, and ask for an invitation to the wedding."

With a laugh, William rushed from behind the desk, hugged his niece, and shook Clayton's hand.

"Thank you, Uncle," Lillian said, wiping tears of happiness from her cheeks.

"Clayton, will you take me back to the house, so I can change clothes before we drive out to Eagle Creek?"

"Sure I will, Lillian, but you look fine to me," Clayton answered.

"Maybe, but when I meet them as your bride-to-be, I want to look my best," Lillian explained.

After another hug and handshake, William walked the couple to the door, and watched them drive away.

~ * ~

While Lillian dressed and arranged her hair, Clayton waited outside by the wagon. After helping her on board, he tied his horse to the back of the wagon and they started out.

"Are you comfortable?" Clayton asked, his brow wrinkled in concern.

Lillian nodded and smiled. She tightened the

bow of her bonnet and inhaled deeply.

Clayton watched the road, and Lillian glanced at him now and then. A quiet settled between them.

"I never thought much about how long it took to ride out to Eagle Creek from town until today," Lillian said, breaking the long silence.

"The excitement of seeing our new home made the first trip seem like an eternity," Clayton recalled. "But I don't think I've ever thought about the distance since then."

"Me neither, until now," Lillian admitted.

"And now?" Clayton looked curiously at his bride-to-be.

"Now Eagle Creek is approaching in the blink of an eye, and I'm getting nervous."

"Lillian, if it'll make you feel any easier, this announcement isn't going to be a shock to the family. I must admit that I discussed this with them thoroughly last night."

"You did?" Lillian sounded both surprised and relieved.

"It was the only fair thing for both you and them. I know how fond they all are of you, but I wasn't sure how they would feel about you becoming a member of the family. It was important that they approve of my idea before I went any farther. I just couldn't bring you into a hostile household, could I?"

"Clayton, what a mess I've made of things. Marriage isn't at all what I once dreamed it would be. When I met David, I had visions of a lacey, white wedding gown, the town in attendance, and doves being released in honor of our marriage. Instead, his family hated me because I wasn't wealthy, or on the social register.

"Now, I'm being wed so that the birth of my

baby won't ruin my uncle's reputation, and brand me a wanton woman. I should be on my knees giving thanks for you and your family, but here I am moaning and groaning because the dreams of my pig-tail days have gone up in smoke. I'm so sorry."

"You know, Lillian, dreams are a part of what makes us different and apart from others. Dreams are what give us hope, and although they can fade away like smoke, new ones can take their place. Losing a dream can be painful, and that pain can make us all moan and groan, but it isn't a death sentence. A faded dream just makes room for another and another."

Lillian entwined her arm with Clayton's. "I swear, Clayton Wilkins, I would have never imagined when I first met you, that you were such a poet. A good-looking, hard-working, knight-in-shining-armor, who knows how to make a lady smile, is a first class bargain if you ask me. What else don't I know about you?"

Clayton's face reddened, and he shook his head. "Not much. I am what you see. And believe me, I'm no bargain. Don't know when it's time for a haircut until one of the children tells me. I don't like wearing a suit, new shoes, or a tie, and don't drink much but now and then I do take a shot. Occasionally, I light up, but generally, I don't smoke. Although hard work is good for the soul, being in debt to anyone gives me sleepless nights. That probably describes most men, more or less."

Lillian laughed. "Remind me to go shopping with you. You don't know a bargain when it's walking in your own shoes."

Clayton gave her a puzzled look, shook his head, and pulled the reins to the left as they approached the drive to Eagle Creek.

~ * ~

"Pa's home, Pa's home," Clay yelled, when he saw the horses come into view. "And Miss Lillian's with him."

"Thank goodness," Mary said. "I was afraid your nose was going to melt into that window pane. You've been staring out that window all morning. Get away from there. You're smearing up the glass, and I'll be the one to have it clean it."

"I saw you lookin' too. I just wanted to see if she was gonna marry Pa."

Mary grinned guiltily. "Yes, you did see me. I was anxious too, but now that I see she's with him, I guess we know the answer."

"We do? How do we know? What did she say?" Clay followed Mary back to the kitchen, pulling on her skirt with every question.

"She said *yes*, silly. If she'd said no, she wouldn't be with him, would she?"

"Why not?" The boy looked at his sister in surprise.

"You just don't understand women," Mary said with a toss of her head. "You're such a child."

"Am not," Clay sniffed with a stamp of his foot. "I know lots of things like taking care of a dog, feeding chickens, cleaning out the barn..."

"Women, I said you don't know anything about women."

"Neither do you. You ain't no woman. You're just a kid, like me."

"Don't say ain't. Sarah will have a fit. And I'm more a woman than you know," she snapped.

She turned and stomped away with her nose in the air. Entering the kitchen, Mary paused dramatically when Irene and Sarah glanced up.

Waving her hand toward the front of the house, she lifted her chin higher, closed her eyes, and said, "They're riding up to the front door as I speak. Papa, that is, and his, um, his new, um-wife-to-be."

Sarah winced at Mary's words but took a deep breath and smiled.

"Good. Now, the waiting is over. If she's with him, that means she's accepted his proposal. Let's get this over with," Sarah grumbled.

This time it was Irene who winced. She furrowed her brow at Sarah's last words. They sounded more like the dread of oncoming punishment than the joy of greeting a future new family member. However, Sarah's smile looked genuine, and hopefully Lillian would be convinced of its sincerity.

The sound of the front door opening, and Clayton's voice, alerted everyone that it was time to welcome Lillian into their home and soon, their family.

"Clay, go get Papa Joe and tell him Lillian's here. If he says he's busy, tell him Gram needs him now. He'll understand." Irene smiled at her grandson when he hesitated at the door. "Go on, now. Papa Joe won't be mad."

"You know when he's busy, he don't like to stop," Clay said, his voice low.

"It's okay. He'll want to know about your Pa and Miss Lillian. Run on."

"Clayton," Irene called. "We're in the kitchen. I've got fresh coffee perking, and the tea kettle is on. Come on back here."

~ * ~

Clay didn't have to worry. As he hopped off the back porch, he saw his grandfather heading toward the house from the barn.

"Papa's back," the boy shouted.

"Is that a fact?" Papa Joe grinned, and ruffled the boy's hair as he passed.

"Yep, it's a fact," Clay said innocently, not hearing the humor in his grandfather's voice.

"Well, come on, boy. We'd getter get in there, or we'll have to hear all about it second-hand, and you know how our womenfolk like to embellish a story."

"What's em-bel-sh mean, Papa Joe?" Clay tilted his head in confusion.

"It means it'll take them twice as long to tell what was said than it would if we were there to hear it firsthand. They'll add fancy words and flower everthin' up so you ain't sure what was really said, and what was just added to make it sound fluffier."

"Fluffier?" The boy still looked confused.

"Never mind, you'll understand when you get older."

"Boy, I bet I'm gonna be real busy when I get older."

"Busy? What makes you say that?"

"'Cause every day I'm told I'm gonna learn something, or know something, or understand something when I get older. It looks like there's a lot to do then."

Joe Martin threw back his head and guffawed, as he guided his frowning grandson through the backdoor into the kitchen.

Mary was putting out cups for the tea and coffee, and glasses for lemonade, when Clayton and Lillian walked side by side into the kitchen. Clayton pulled out a chair for his new fiancé.

"Hey, Miss Lillian, how are you today?" Joe asked, then leaned over to peck his wife on the cheek.

"I'm fine, thank you, Mister Martin."

"If what I'm thinking is true, I guess you'd better start calling me Joe," he said.

"No sense in playing games," Clayton said with a smile. "Lillian has just consented to be my wife. I guess we'll be having a wedding around here fairly soon."

"Oh, my dear, welcome to our family," Irene said. She stood, went to Lillian and hugged her.

"Yes, welcome," Sarah said, her voice low.

"Do I have to call you *Ma*?" Clay looked at his father, and then at Lillian.

Before Clayton could speak, Lillian rose, went to the boy, and squatted down in front of him. She reached out and touched his cheek with her fingertips.

"Clay," she said gently. "No one can take the place of your mother. I'm going to be you father's wife, and hopefully a friend to you, Mary, and Sarah. Marrying your father will legally make me a member of your family, but only your acceptance will make it true. I know it will take time for that to happen, but I'm up to it if you are. I think for now, just calling me *Lillian* will do. That's what friends do."

Clay thought for a moment and then he grinned. "Papa Joe once told me you can't ever have too many friends. I'm glad you're marrying Pa. Sometimes I think he gets lonely."

Sarah's head jerked up at her brother's wise observation. She had never thought of her father being lonely, but it made perfect sense. She, of all the children, remembered how close her parents had been, and how much happier Clayton had been before her mother died. Of course, he missed Susan. She had been his best friend, his partner, his confidant. Now that he had Lillian, it might not be exactly the same, but it could be a good thing. As long as he didn't have to worry about his children's acceptance, he could have a wonderful relationship with Lillian. She smiled and stepped forward.

"Lillian, I'm glad you're going to be a member of our family. We've all liked you from the beginning, and I think, like you said, time will blend us into a real family."

Tears pooled in Lillian's eyes. She put her hand on Sarah's shoulder.

"I appreciate your kindness. I know this can't be easy."

"When's the wedding?" Mary asked, seeming oblivious to the emotions flowing between Sarah and Lillian.

"Yeah, when?" Clay Junior echoed.

"Well, the decision is between Lillian and your father, of course," Irene said slowly. "But I think the sooner, the better. With all the work we have ahead of us, and winter on the way, Lillian will want to get settled in as soon as possible."

"Yes... of course, you're right," Lillian said.

She smiled gratefully at Irene for giving them an easily accepted reason for a quick wedding.

"Lillian, the final decision is yours, of course. I want you to be happy."

"I know you do, Clayton, and I want that for you as well. We're all invested in this decision, and it affects us all. I want a small family wedding, and

I'd like it to be here, if that's all right with you. Except for the minister, I only want Uncle William and all of you here," Lillian said.

"This lovely house would be a perfect setting. Of course, it's all right with us. If the weather is good, the back garden could be fixed up for the ceremony and we could have the reception here in the house." Irene looked around at the smiles on the children's faces.

"Oh, please, don't go to any trouble," Lillian pleaded. She looked from Clayton to Irene.

"Child, this is right up Irene's alley," Joseph assured her. "You'll understand what I'm talking about when you see how she decorates the house for Thanksgiving and Christmas."

Irene smiled shyly at her husband's remark. "Life can become tedious and boring if you don't make the most of special occasions," she said. "Having something exciting on the horizon gives us all something to look forward to. Don't you agree?"

"How soon is *soon as possible*?" Clay asked with a frown on his face. "Why don't you just say tomorrow or next Sunday? *Soon* is kinda like saying *maybe* or *we'll see*? It don't tell you nuttin'." He looked at his grandmother, his lips pursed.

"H-rummp," Joseph snorted, looking as if he was trying not to laugh.

Everyone turned to Clayton and Lillian.

"Well... I don't want the date to put any pressure on anyone, or set back any work that needs to be done." Lillian turned and gazed into Clayton's eyes.

"You pick the date, Lillian and I'll make sure there's no pressure, and no work is neglected. Don't forget, we have Daniel here to lend a hand."

"Irene, do... do you think two weeks from next Saturday will be too soon?" Lillian asked shyly.

"Two weeks from next Saturday will be perfect."

"Isn't that a little too soon?" Sarah stiffened and glared at her grandmother.

"Well," Irene glanced coyly at her husband, who stood silent. "As I recall, your grandfather and I married just about two weeks after he proposed. I guess once you've made the decision to marry, there isn't a *too soon*. It seemed to work out okay for us, don't you think?"

"I guess." Sarah relaxed, and watched her grandparents gaze into one another's eyes.

"Sarah?" Lillian took Sarah's hand. "I wonder if you would be my maid of honor. You're the closest thing I have to a best friend."

Sarah blinked hard and stared at Lillian. "You... you want me?"

"It would make me very happy if you would. I can understand if you don't want to, but..."

"Yes," Sarah said. "Yes, I would love to. Thank you for asking."

"I'm going to ask Uncle William to walk me down the aisle. And Mary, I'd like you to be my bridesmaid, if you will."

"Of course, I will," Mary squealed, revealing the joy of being included.

"What about me?" Clay asked sullenly.

"Why, I guess you'll have to be the best man," Clayton said with a smile.

"What's a best man? I thought the groom was the best man?" The boy looked at his father.

"Well, the best man is the fellow the groom trusts to hold the wedding ring until it's time to put it on his bride's finger," Clayton explained.

"It's really an honor," Joseph added.

"Wow," Clay said. "That's great."

"Okay, you people. Talking time is over. Clayton, you can get out of those Sunday-go-to meetin'-clothes. I know you can't wait. You men get on back to work. We ladies have a lot to talk about.

"Mary, see if the kettle's hot. Sarah, see if there are any molasses cookies left. Lillian and I need to settle on how we want this shindig to go. Run on now and get busy."

~ * ~

Daniel was relieved that his nights had been undisturbed by chills, mists or sounds. He was still bothered by dreams of a sailing ship floundering in a storm, by barroom fights, and bitter arguments that he couldn't quite understand. Still, the dreams were less often. He had settled into the little cabin, and Irene and the girls had worked hard to make it comfortable and homey.

He, along with Joseph and Clayton, had repaired the roof, chinked up the logs and filled all the cracks around the windows and doors. The stove had been cleaned and polished, and he was able to have coffee in the late evening after work, when he could relax and enjoy the quiet.

Now, all thoughts were on the upcoming wedding. Daniel didn't know why, but he was happy for Clayton. He had never had a family before, and his feelings confused him.

~ * ~

Lillian and Irene spent almost every waking hour together, between chores, and trips back and forth to town. It was no surprise that tongues wagged about some of the things the ladies bought, but no one had any concrete piece of gossip to share.

Mary and Sarah tied bows and added sprigs of wildflowers, placing bouquets above each doorway, and on the backs of the chairs in the dining room, and on the first chair of each row outside, leading up to the alter.

Lillian found her mother's wedding dress and with a few alterations here and there, Irene fitted it perfectly for the bride-to-be. Joseph, Clayton, and Clay brushed their suits and polished their shoes in preparation for the big day.

William spoke with Reverend Talley, and when he explained that Clayton and Lillian wanted the ceremony to be private and unannounced, he agreed.

The big day arrived and William drove Lillian to Eagle Creek. For the ride, she wore a simple, blue gingham dress. Her wedding gown, shoes, and veil had been packed in the buggy before dawn. Neither of them spoke a word on the road, and only when William turned into the drive, did Lillian break the silence.

"Thank you, Uncle William." Lillian's eyes began to tear.

"For what?" William asked. "Child, I'm so happy for you and Clayton. I think this is a match made in heaven. I'm proud to give you away, and see my precious niece walk down the aisle and become the wife of such a fine man."

Lillian slipped her arm under his and laid her head on his shoulder.

As they approached the house, William

nudged his niece, and Lillian's face lit up. William looked just as happy.

White ribbons, topped with lovely bows, decorated the front of the house.

Clay held the team, while William and Lillian climbed down. He then led the wagon around back, where Daniel took over.

Inside, lamps and candles illuminated the hallway, and led down the hall, to the back door.

Irene stepped out of the parlor, dressed in her best beige, lace dress. Her silver hair shone in the lamplight, and her smile added to the glow of the occasion.

"Oh, Irene, it's all so beautiful." Lillian turned slowly, admiring the glittering flames.

"This is your day, my dear. I wanted it to be beautiful for you. Come on back to the bedroom, and let's get you dressed. The preacher should be here any minute. Joseph has gone to pick him up. William, you wait here in the parlor. Daniel and Clayton will be in shortly."

"Yes, ma'am," William replied, and straightened his waistcoat as he stepped into the parlor.

Before he could make himself comfortable, he glanced out the window and saw Joseph pulling up the drive with Reverend Talley by his side.

"Whoa," he murmured and exhaled heavily. "It's really happening."

"You okay, Mister Gaines?" Clay walked in and looked at his soon-to-be-step-uncle.

"Please, Clay," William said. "Call me Uncle William. After all, we're about to become related, sort of, aren't we?"

"Yeah, Uncle William, I guess we are." Clay looked around, grinned sheepishly, and shrugged.

"This stuff is brand new to me. I'm not sure what I'm supposed to do."

"Son, this is new to me, too. I wouldn't worry though. I'm sure someone will be along soon and tell us where to go, what to do, and how to do it. When you've got several women in charge of a shindig, there's always someone who will tell us what to do."

"Don't I know it," Clay said, his shoulders drooped, and his face fell. "Someone is always bossin' me around and telling me what to do. I guess you've been there, too."

"You're right about that. I was raised in a household of women like you. Between my grand-mother, my mother, and my sister, I got ordered around like you do, too. But one thing I learned, was all that bossing teaches you to be patient, alert, and aware of what needs to be done, what's important, and how to take directions. One day, Son, you'll re-alize that all the bossing was nothing more than les-sons. You'll thank them. Wait and see."

"Maybe," Clay said. His brow furrowed and his lips pursed. "Maybe I will, but right now it just seems like bossin'"

"Ah-hem." Clayton cleared his throat when he entered the parlor.

"Wow, Pa, you surely do look fancy," the boy said admiringly, and looked his father up and down.

"Is that good?" Clayton replied nervously, glancing down at his suit and shoes.

"Yes, that's good," Sarah answered, coming in behind him. "In fact, you look as handsome as the bride looks beautiful. She just finished dressing, Pa, and she's a vision."

"Where is everybody?" Joseph called from the hallway. "I thought we were gonna have a wedding today. Has everybody changed their minds?"

Reverend Talley, who was standing behind Joseph, wore a wide smile that creased his sun-tanned, weather-worn face.

"I imagine everyone is taking care of last minute details, Joe," he said, resting his hand on Joseph's shoulder.

"Don't know why we couldn't have brought you out, had you say the proper words, and got on back to business," Joe said loudly, peering down the hall toward the back bedroom. He turned and winked at the Reverend.

"For heaven's sake, Joseph, lower your voice. We're just about ready, and nobody, and I mean nobody, wants to hear the words and get on back to business. This is a special time and it calls for special attitudes." Irene stood outside the bedroom door, her hands on her ample hips.

"Simmer down, woman, and don't get so riled up. I was funnin' you. Can't you take a joke?" Joseph said with a smile.

"Oh, well... Hello Reverend Talley. Thank you so much for coming," Irene said.

"It's my pleasure, Mrs. Martin. I've known Lillian since she was born. I am honored to preside at her wedding. I've no doubt this union was made in heaven."

Clayton walked to the door when he heard them talking. He glanced upward and smiled.

"They have no idea, do they, Susan?" He whispered.

Within a few minutes, the group was outdoors. Irene and the girls had placed several chairs by the pond, and ribbons and bows decorated the small area where the ceremony would take place. Reverend Talley stood in the front, with Clayton and Clay on his left, while Joseph, Irene, and Daniel sat in the chairs.

Mary walked out the back door, proceeded down the aisle, and stood on the preacher's right. She held her small, white Bible in her hand, cleared her throat, and looked at her family. In a clear, angelic voice, she began to sing *Amazing Grace*. The words poured out into the bright, sunny garden, filled with peace and comfort.

When the last note faded away, the back door opened again and Sarah exited, dressed in her Sunday best, and walked down the aisle. When she reached the front, she stood next to her sister. Then everyone turned toward the house.

The door opened again, and Lillian, on the arm of her uncle, walked slowly toward Reverend Talley and Clayton.

Clay tugged on his father's pant leg. "Don't she look purdy, Pa?" His eyes danced with excitement.

"Yes, she does," Clayton answered.

Lillian's mother's dress fit her perfectly, with layers of white muslin cascading from her waist to the floor. Her hair had been put up in a mass of curls, and a sheer veil covered her face, held in place by a crown of braided daisies. Her bouquet was a medley of wildflowers, held together by streamers of ribbons, hanging almost to the hem of her dress. Regardless of the necessity of this wedding, both bride and groom looked confident and proud.

When they reached the front, William placed

Lillian's hand in Clayton's, and Clayton gave her a gentle squeeze. Lillian smiled shyly, turned, and handed her bouquet to Mary.

Reverend Talley cleared his throat, smiled at the couple, and began the ceremony. Clay smiled broadly, handed his father the ring when given the signal, and stepped back to watch Clayton slip the plain gold band onto Lillian's finger. The minister concluded the service, and pronounced them husband and wife. Clayton tenderly kissed his bride. Everyone applauded and laughed when Clayton and Lillian both ducked their heads and blushed.

"All right y'all. The deed is done. Let's get inside and chow down. Bob here rushed me through breakfast, and my stomach has been complaining ever since," Joseph announced, while heading toward the kitchen door.

"Papa Joe has the right idea. We've been cooking, baking, and fixing for this celebration all week. Let's go in," Sarah said, following her grandfather, and motioning to the others.

The gathering for the big event may have been small, but Robbie Irene Martin prepared an amazing feast. Plates and platters of steaming, delicious-smelling dishes covered the table and sideboard.

There were piles of cold sliced chicken and ham, bowls of steaming corn on the cob, containers of potato salad, plates of sliced tomatoes, cucumbers, pickled beets and squash, and baskets of fresh, sliced, homemade bread. Large pitchers of sweet tea, ice water, and lemonade sat on the buffet, surrounded by slices of lemon and sprigs of mint.

It may not have been the fine cuisine wealthy

families served at their society weddings, but it was good, old-fashioned, comfort food that soothed the soul and relaxed those present. Soon, laughter and gaiety filled the old mansion of Eagle Creek Farm, and hope grew in the hearts of all those present.

~ TEN ~
New Beginning, New Friends

From the first moment they met, the Martins and Wilkins' made Lillian feel comfortable and at ease. Now that she was a member of the family, that feeling continued. She woke the next morning and saw Clayton washing his face in the dressing room. He turned around to see her watching him, and he grinned shyly.

"Morning, Mrs. Clayton Wilkins."

"Good morning, Mister Clayton Wilkins," she replied with a smile.

Fastening his suspenders, her new husband put his arms into the blue chambray shirt he had chosen for the day.

Throwing back the covers, Lillian slipped into her robe, and hurried to the closet where just the day before, she, Sarah, and Mary had hung up the clothes she brought. Pulling out a blue-gray dress trimmed in lace, she glanced out the window, noticing the position of the sun.

"Oh, my, Clayton, it's late. Irene and Joseph must think me the laziest woman on earth. How could I have slept so late? If you're finished, please give me a chance to dress. I won't be but a minute. What must they think of me?"

She rushed toward the dressing room, but Clayton stepped in front of her, and gently held her by the shoulders.

"Lillian, surely you don't think they are sitting downstairs judging their new daughter-in-law by what time she wakes up the morning after she is newly married?" he asked. His grin widened, and he gazed into her eyes. "In fact, Joseph suggested yesterday that you and I take the day and relax, but I reminded him that winter is coming, and I'd like to get as much firewood cut as we can manage."

Lillian looked at her new husband, noticing the way he studied her. She relaxed, took a few deep breaths, and when she felt her pounding heart slow to a normal beat, returned his grin.

"I wanted to make a good impression by being on time when Irene arrived in the kitchen. Guess I missed that opportunity."

"Guess so," he said jokingly. "Actually, I've discovered that Irene likes a little time alone when she first gets to the kitchen. I tried to help her out the first morning we were here, and she hustled me out faster than a jackrabbit. She has her own agenda when she starts the day, but once she's had that first cup of coffee, she's as gentle as a lamb."

"I'll try to remember that," Lillian nodded. "I bet she's already had that cup this morning, and I don't want her thinking me a slacker."

Pushing past him, she dressed in a hurry, and twisted her hair up, while walking back into the bed-room.

"You look real nice, Lillian."

Clayton reached over, took her hand, and gave her an encouraging smile and a quick kiss, then opened the door to the hallway.

She was greeted warmly by the family who made her feel she had always been a member, and the day passed quickly. Lillian learned the sched-ules, chores, and easy but steady, life of the Wil-kins'. Days melted one into the other, and Lillian grew more relaxed and comfortable.

The days faded into weeks, and the weeks in-to months. Lillian stayed busy mending the children's clothes, and remaking a couple of her old dresses for Sarah, while re-fitting Sarah's outgrown clothes for Mary. School started in a couple of weeks, and Lillian wanted the girls to have new clothes. She and Irene made Clay several new shirts, but he still needed sturdy pants from the General Store.

Classes started later in Sycamore Grove than in Dawson City, due to the harvest and canning season. All families needed their children home to help. Lillian and Clayton loaded up the children in the wagon, and drove into town so Lillian could talk to the schoolmistress, Miss Gretchen Schmitz.

Clayton dropped Lilllian and the children at the schoolhouse, and drove down the street to the general store.

"Good morning, Miss Schmitz," Lillian said, entering the schoolhouse. "I'm Lillian Wilkins, and this is Sarah, Mary, and Clay Wilkins. This will be their first school year here in Sycamore Grove. I've filled out their registration papers I picked up earlier. I wanted to bring the papers by and introduce ourselves."

"I've seen all of you around town before, and hoped to meet you." The teacher smiled at the children, and handed each of them a peppermint stick.

"We have some new playground equipment," Miss Schmitz said to the children. "Perhaps you'd like to go outside and look at the swings and see-saw while Miss Lillian and I talk?"

"Yes, ma'am, we surely would," Clay said. "Mary, will you swing me?"

Mary smiled, took his hand, and followed Sarah outside.

"The children are a little nervous about starting a new school," Lillian explained. "I just wanted to make sure they were going to be comfortable here."

"Don't worry, Miss Lillian. I remember how l frightened I was, and how much I missed my old friends when I first arrived from Norway. When I became a teacher, I made a vow that none of my students would feel lonely. I'll take good care of them, I promise," the young teacher assured her.

Lillian smiled and glanced out the window. "Their father and I haven't been married long, and the children and I are still bonding. I don't want anything to get in the way of their happiness if I can help it. It's hard for them having to adjust to so many new changes in their lives in such a short period of time."

"I'm so glad you came by. I'll make sure their school days go by as smoothly as possible. Between the two of us, your children are going to be fine, I assure you," Miss Schmitz said. "Let me give you the list of supplies they'll need and their books. Maybe they'll like practicing before classes start."

"Thank you, if there is anything we can do at home to help them, please let us know."

Lillian walked outside and called the children. "Let's go meet your father. I have a list of the supplies you'll need. We can pick them up early."

"Yippee," cried Clay. "Let's go git 'em."

"That sounds great," Sarah said. "You definitely need some lessons, especially in English."

This was the last trip Lillian would make into town until after the baby was born. She barely showed, and was still able to hide her condition beneath loose clothing.

Lillian and the children entered the store, and while Lillian joined Clayton, the children began examining everything on the shelves.

"How did it go at the school?" Clayton asked.

"Just fine. I think the children will adapt well, and I really like the new teacher, Miss Schmitz. She gave me a list of supplies the children need." She handed the list to Clayton. "I'm going to see about some sewing supplies Irene mentioned she needs."

Clayton glanced at the list and handed it to Robert Barker. They continued their conversation, while Robert's son, Nate, filled the boxes.

Lillian walked around, pausing in the corner, to pick out a few spools of thread. Then she felt a light touch on her arm.

"Mrs. Wilkins, you may not remember me. I'm Elsie Barker. My husband owns the store." A soft, gentle voice spoke from behind her.

Turning, Lillian saw a tiny, pale woman nervously plucking at her hands, though she was smiling.

"Of course, I remember you, Mrs. Barker. It's been a while," Lillian answered.

"Yes, I'm easy to forget," the woman replied.

"Not at all," Lillian said quickly.

"Oh, don't apologize. It's just that people generally frighten me. They always have. I'm no good working in the store. But Nathaniel's so good to me. He understands how it is, and lets me do the ordering and bookkeeping. That lets me feel useful, and I don't have to face many customers.

"But you... I felt drawn to you somehow. It's strange because that doesn't happen often." She paused and looked at her hands.

"When are you due?" she whispered softly.

"W-what?" Lillian stammered, and stared at the woman.

"I'm sorry," Elsie said quickly. "Don't be offended. I'll leave you alone."

Lillian reached out and held her wrist. "No, please. I'm not offended, just startled. How did you know? Does it show that much?"

"Oh no, not at all, it's just that... I always know. I don't know why or how. My Grannie knew, too, and I just know." She lowered her eyes and looked as if she were ready to bolt.

"Miss Elsie, would you like to have a cup of tea with me at the sweet shop, while my husband finishes the buying?" Lillian reached out, took Elsie's chin in her hand, and raised her face to look into her eyes.

The tiny women smiled shyly and nodded. "Yes, I would. Let me get my hat and shawl."

Nathaniel Barker looked stunned when he saw his wife leaving the store, arm-in-arm with Lillian Wilkins.

Clayton looked at him and grinned. "You look a little startled, Nathaniel. Is there a problem?"

Nathaniel quickly recovered and returned the grin.

"Absolutely not, in fact, I'm delighted. You see..." he paused and lowered his voice. "Elsie is a timid soul, very shy and reserved. I met her in Boston when I went to visit friends shortly after I graduated business school. She was like a fawn—tiny, delicate, and so lovely. However, she froze around most people, and simply couldn't hold a conversation. It didn't matter to me. We seemed to be a perfect match. She had no problem talking to me, and I could see she was a very special person. I worried about how she would cope in a public life like I have here at the store.

"But she tries, she really does. She does the ordering, takes care of the books, and pays all the bills. She's a wonder, she is, but she doesn't make friends easily. She slips in and out of church like a ghost, doesn't belong to any social groups, or the garden club, and doesn't have any friends to speak of. So when I saw her leave on your wife's arm, well, I was surprised. Delighted, of course, but surprised." He still stared at the door that had shut behind his wife and Lillian.

"Lillian can tame the wildest beast, and comfort the most timid soul," Clayton bragged. "She's a prize, that woman is. Perhaps they'll become friends. You and your family are welcome at Eagle Creek anytime. Please make it a point to come by."

"We will, I assure you," Nathaniel said, sounding proud and pleased.

At the tea shop, the tea and cakes were delivered. Elsie insisted on paying, and when the waitress left, she glanced around and looked out the window.

Lillian sipped her tea, allowing Elsie to gather her thoughts.

"I've only been here one other time," Elise said softly. "Nat and I were newly married, and had just arrived in town. I'd never met his family. Our courtship and marriage was a whirlwind affair, and I was terrified they wouldn't like me. He brought me here for a strong cup of tea before taking me to the store to meet his family."

"That must have been so hard," Lillian sympathized.

"It was," Elsie whispered. "But it shouldn't have been. I just seem to make things harder for myself. They were concerned of course, but they couldn't have been kinder. After a few stiff minutes, Nat's father slapped his knee and told a joke. I giggled. Frances, his mother, smiled, and they both welcomed me with open arms.

"They were the only friends I had. When they died, I felt as if I had lost my own parents again. I was orphaned at ten, and raised as a ward of my uncle when I first met Nat.

"Please, forgive me. I don't know what came over me. I've never exposed so much of my life to a complete stranger before. I've completely monopolized the conversation." Elsie covered her face with her hands and trembled.

"Elsie, please relax. I feel so honored that you've confided in me. I lost my parents, too, but I had Uncle William. Still, like you, I've never had any friends outside the family. I can't imagine your grief of having lost both sets of parents. I would be devastated. I am so sorry for your tragic loss."

"Thank you for your kindness. Our son, Nathan, helps Robert in the store every day after school, and on Saturdays. He really is a good boy. We're very proud of him.

"I believe our children are gifts, and we must do all we can for them. Our job is not to be friends, but to be guides for them while they are young," Elsie said, dabbing her mouth with a delicate, lace handkerchief, and picked up her tea.

"Speaking of children, I almost forgot," Elsie said, setting her cup back down. "When did you say your arrival was due?"

Lillian's face lit up. She dabbed her lips with the napkin, and said softly, "Around the end of December, if I'm not mistaken."

Elsie reached over and touched Lillian's hand. She closed her eyes for a moment and smiled. "Better sew several extra gifts for Christmas. I don't think you will wait that long."

Lillian stiffened. "Are you sure?" she gasped.

Elsie nodded, and gazed into her new friend's eyes. "You must tell the little boy. He's worried about you."

"Clay? I never realized he was concerned." Lillian's eyes filled with tears. "I must admit that I'm a little concerned. Will he, or she, be healthy?"

Elsie smiled even wider. "Yes," she said firmly. "The birth...," she paused again, seeming to hide a secretive smile, "will be just fine."

"How long have you... could you...?" Lillian's voice faltered while she searched for the right words.

Elsie smiled knowingly. "I've had the sight as long as I can remember. That's one of the reasons I have no friends. When I was younger, everyone thought I was mad, and the neighbor children were not allowed to play with *crazy Elsie*. Even my aunt and uncle forbid me to speak of things they said I knew nothing about.

"I eventually closed myself off from the world. Only when Nathaniel entered my life was I able to hope that, at last, I'd found someone who would accept me as I am. He did. I've been so blessed. You're the first person in years that I felt comfortable in revealing myself to."

"I am so grateful that you did. I feel we're

going to be great friends. Please arrange to come spend the day at our home. I want you to meet my family and get acquainted." Lillian sipped her tea, and glanced out the window.

"Thank you for the tea. I see my husband and children by the wagon. I'm sure he's ready to get back home. I know you're very busy in your duties at the store, but perhaps next week I could expect you?" Lillian asked with a smile.

"Would Wednesday be acceptable?"

"I will be waiting for you Wednesday morning. Don't forget."

Lillian rose, adjusted her shawl, and took Elsie's arm. Together they walked out of the tea shop.

"How could I forget? I've dreamed of this meeting, time and time again." Elsie smiled.

~ * ~

Elsie became a regular visitor to Eagle Creek Farm. The family fell in love with her shy nature and gentle smile. She never failed to bring sweets for the children and a bone for Honey. She often brought a basket of tiny coffee cakes for the ladies to serve with their tea and coffee. Irene taught Elsie to crochet, and they sat for hours making tiny baby garments.

Early one morning, Lillian took Clay for a long walk on the pretense of gathering pecans for the holidays. She wanted a quiet place to inform him of the arrival of the new family member.

"Here," Clay called to Lillian. "There's some real big 'uns over here. Pa calls 'em paper shell pecans 'cause they're so big, and the shell is paper thin, and easy to break. Watch, I can put two in my hand and mash with my other hand, and they'll just break apart."

"That's wonderful, Clay. Your grandmother wants to bake a pecan pie, and put some in cakes and cookies." Lillian held out the basket and Clay dumped his hand full of nuts inside.

"Clay, what do you think of having a new baby sister or brother some day?" Lillian asked, watching her step-son scoop up nuts.

"I wouldn't be the youngest anymore, would I?" Clay looked at Lillian, a wide smile on his face.

"No you wouldn't. You'd be the big brother, and the baby would look to you to show him or her all the things you know. You could help teach the baby to talk, walk, and eat with a spoon..."

"...and I could teach him to take care of Honey, feed the chickens, play tag, go fishing, and climb trees." Clay looked at Lillian. "He could help gather pecans, too, couldn't he?"

"Well, yes, but the baby might be a girl, and she might want to have tea parties, and play with dolls. Would you still like a baby in the family if she were a girl?"

"I would rather have a brother, but I could teach a baby sister some really neat things. Albert has a baby cousin name named Sally Mae, and she's just learning to walk. Every time I go to his house, Sally Mae follows us all over the place. She's kinda cute. Albert and me are trying to teach her to whistle" Clay paused and laughed. "She can't whistle yet, but she tries."

Lillian smiled. "I'm glad you like Sally, and wouldn't mind having a sister." Lillian squatted down and took Clay's hand. "We are going to have a baby in the family around Christmas, and you'll be a wonderful big brother."

"Christmas," Clay said and laughed. "I'll have a baby brother or sister around Christmas? Oh, boy, wait 'til I tell Albert—a baby—oh, boy. I won't be the baby anymore. Watcha gonna name him, oops, or her? Didja tell Pa, yet? Where's the baby gonna sleep? We'll have to pick out a good room. What does a baby eat?" Clay rattled off the questions while running around, picking up pecans.

"We have a lot of details to work out between now and then, that's for sure," Lillian said with a smile. "You and the girls will help us decide, I'm sure."

"Sure we'll help. This'll be fun. Is this enough pecans?" Clay asked, looking in the basket.

"That's plenty. Let's go home." Lillian rested her hand on Clay's shoulder, and looked into his smiling face.

Clay nodded, and the two of them started back to the house.

~*~

Daniel, Joseph, and Clayton finished plowing all the fields under, winterized all the out-buildings, and continued to cut wood for the cook stove and fireplace.

The skies became sunless, gray, ominous, and the last trip to town was scheduled.

Snow was predicted, so the men laid a partial stone floor in a corner of the barn. They wanted to install a small wood stove there, in order to protect the barn from the freezing weather.

School was underway, and by seven o'clock each morning, the children climbed into the wagon for the drive to town.

Winter was a time for rest, a time for regeneration, a time to plan, dream, and make decisions for the spring.

~*~

Daniel spent more and more time in the main house. The temperature had dropped into the thirties, and the wind felt sharp as a knife, cutting through the tiniest hole or crack. Although Daniel kept a fire going in the little stove in his cabin, being alone just added to the chill outside.

Clayton talked to Lillian, then in turn, discussed their idea with Irene and Joseph. They all decided to fix up a small room off the kitchen for Daniel.

Daniel protested, but eventually had to agree that it was becoming impossible to keep the little cabin warm. Besides, he was secretly pleased that he would be inside the big house. Try as he might, he had not been able to devise a plan that gave him any reason to be there. Things were finally falling into place.

He was given use of the library, sitting room, kitchen, and it was in the library that he ran into Sarah. She sat curled up by the fireplace reading, completely unaware he was watching.

"Is that a good book?" He asked.

She jumped and grinned.

"Didn't mean to scare you," he said softly.

"Oh, you didn't, you just startled me," she answered.

"Is it?" He asked.

"Is what it?" she said, brows knitted together, and her head tilted to one side.

"Is it a good book?" He said slowly, his hands moving comically while he mimed each word in a made-up sign language.

She laughed. "Yes, very, but it's not a book. It's a journal written by the woman who used to live here."

His heart lurched. "I thought a guy named Kaymey lived here?" He could hardly prevent his lips from trembling.

"Well, we thought so, too, at first. I showed this to Grandma, and she's not sure I should believe what's written here. She thinks it might be a joke. But listen, I found some newspapers in the cellar that proves what the woman wrote is true.

"Wait here. Let me go get them." She jumped up and ran out of the room, hurrying up the stairs.

Daniel was in shock. It had been months since he arrived, and had spent weeks planning his search, and hopeful discovery. Now that he was in the house, everything was falling into his lap. It made him nervous, though. It appeared too easy, and things that were too easy could be dangerous. His granddaddy taught him that.

Before he could finish his thoughts, Sarah was back, spreading newspapers across the floor.

"See," she said excitedly. "Here are all the accounts of the sinking of the Central America. That was the ship the writer of the journal says she was on. You have to read it, Daniel.

"She met a lovely, old gentleman on board who had no family. Because of his dress and his odd ways, passengers and crew were rude, and dismissed him. She felt sorry for him, bought him some tea, and they became fast friends.

"Just before the ship went down, he insisted that this woman take his gold-filled money belt, and his carpet bag, which was also filled with gold. Hundreds and hundreds of men drowned, but the women and children were all saved, and she survived with the man's money-belt and carpet bag.

"Daniel, the woman who wrote this diary describes how frightened she was of the man she thought she once loved. He lied about marrying her, stole her mother's inheritance and jewels, except for some that she hid, and he beat her when he was broke and got drunk.

"She told how she cut her hair, bought men's clothes, and disguised herself as a man to prevent people from knowing who she really was. She was so ashamed of what had happened to her."

Daniel's ears began to ring and he felt the room sway. "Did she say why she changed her appearance? Who was she hiding from? What had she done?"

Sarah picked up the book tenderly. "I think she wanted to make the foolish girl she once was, disappear. She was hiding from the man who had betrayed and abused her. She hadn't done anything wrong, except fall in love with a monster."

"L-love," he stammered.

"Yes, here let me read you something."

She fanned several pages, slowly turned a couple more, then backed up a page.

"Listen to this," she said softly.

> *The hurt and humiliation I felt from Marcus' betrayal has faded. I guess time does that so we don't suffer our entire life from a broken heart. The pain he caused me both physically and mentally becomes harder and harder to remember, and his tender touch and sweet words become easier to recall.*

Bobbie Shafer

I did love Marcus Alexander, and the joy I felt when I thought he loved me brings a sad smile.

Weakness of the heart is not always a physical condition, sometimes it is a state of mind. I repeat, I did love Marcus, but I only loved the man I thought he was, and not the man that hid behind the mask. I was too blind to see the person he really was.

I still dream of love, even if it's just temporary.

It leaves such memories... and you only remember the good times.

"Oh, Daniel, isn't that romantic? This man seduced and betrayed her. He practically kidnapped her, stole her inheritance, gambled it away, beat her, abandoned her in a strange place, and all she can remember is that she loved him.

"She changed her appearance so that her family would never find her. She was so ashamed of having dishonored her family name, and couldn't bear disgracing her father and brother anymore."

Daniel felt as if he was suffocating. He couldn't breathe. With his hand to his throat, he reached out with his other one, and felt his way along the wall. The scene before his eyes began to swim and waver.

"Daniel," Sarah screamed when she looked up. "Grandma, Papa, come quick, something's wrong with Daniel."

He fought for control. He concentrated on his breathing. *Slowly, he thought, Breathe slowly, close your eyes, get a grip.* He leaned over, put his head between his knees and slid down the wall.

In his mind he could hear his grandfather's words.

"I loved that woman," he had said. *"I wanted to convince her father that I was the right man for his daughter, but she wouldn't wait. She insisted that we run away. I spent months on my hands and knees panning for gold to make a good life for Aimee, and the minute my back was turned, she stole it all and ran away with my best friend.*

"I heard she took his money, too, and left him like she left me. I'll not rest until she's paid for destroying my life, and the future I could have given you and your father. I had a fortune, boy. I had enough gold to set you up for life, and she took it from me.

"Your father was weak and foolish. He turned away from the mission I set for him. He married a woman as weak as he was. She couldn't handle his gambling and drinking. Her death was due to sorrow... sorrow for the dream she never saw fulfilled. Your father drank himself to death because he was weak... too weak to carry on the quest for revenge.

"All of this is that woman's fault, that Aimee McKay. She stole your future, and killed mine. We must have retribution, Daniel. Only then can I rest, knowing your future is secure."

A cool feeling eased his feverish thoughts. The dizziness passed, and soon, he could discern voices.

"Daniel, can you hear me?" A woman's soft voice asked. "Daniel, open your eyes."

He felt a soft cloth being drawn across his forehead, across his mouth.

"Should we call the doctor?" a masculine voice asked.

Daniel forced his eyes open, and shook his head. "No, no, I'll be all right. No doctor, please."

"Here, drink this," Lillian ordered, and pressed a cool china cup to his lips.

The warm liquid trickled down his throat, and throughout his body. He took a deep breath and struggled to sit up, pushing the cup away.

"Easy, son," Joseph said. "Maybe this would help more."

He poured a little brandy between Daniel's lips. Daniel coughed as the strong liquid ran down. He took another deep breath and smiled.

"I don't know what that was all about." He grinned weakly, and shook his head.

"Clayton, you and Joseph help him to his room, and get him in bed. I'll make some strong tea, and bring in some chicken broth. Maybe he just isn't eating well enough," Lillian suggested, and Irene nodded in agreement.

"Could be just a winter sickness. You know, change in the air and temperature," Joseph said.

He and Clayton hoisted Daniel between them and headed for his room.

After Joseph and Clayton had taken Daniel to his room, and Lillian and Irene had gone to the kitchen, the Mary and Clay went into the library, and sat beside Sarah, who was pale and shaky.

"What happened, Sarah?" Clay asked, sinking to the floor.

"I'm not sure," Sarah answered. "I was reading to him from the journal, and those newspapers I found, and when I looked up, he was reeling about and his eyes were rolling around. I thought he was dying."

"You read him those newspapers?" Clay asked, incredulously.

"What's wrong with that?" Mary said, looking from Clay to Sarah.

"She just acted so secretive in the cellar the day she found them. We thought she found some kind of mystery story." Clay stared at his sister.

"I have acted a little silly," Sarah said. "I might as well tell you. I found this diary in the library one night. The owner of this house was not a man at all, but a woman disguised as a man.

"Mack Kaymey wasn't the owner's real name, it was Aimee McKay. The diary tells an incredible story of how she ran away with this man who promised to marry her, but he spent all her money, beat her, and discarded her like an old shoe. She sold a piece of her late mother's jewelry that she hid under a loose board in the cabin, and bought a ticket to sail to New York.

"In Panama they transferred to a paddle-wheel steamship called the S.S. Central America, and it sailed into a hurricane. An old man she befriended on board couldn't swim, and knew he was going to die. He was grateful for her friendship, and insisted Aimee McKay take his gold-filled money belt and carpet bag.

"She and all the other women and children were put into lifeboats and rescued. Aimee changed her appearance and her name, and ended up here."

"Why in the world haven't you told us this before?" Mary asked. "This is a better story than I ever read in a book."

"I don't know," Sarah said sheepishly. "Clay had a new dog and a new friend. You seemed to be in your own little world, happy and busy. I just felt a little left out, and it was kinda fun knowing something exciting and mysterious that nobody else knew. I should have told you. It would have been fun sharing, but I didn't, and I'm sorry."

"Well, we know now," Clay said, trying to mend Mary's feelings.

Mary slumped lower on the floor, her shoulders sagging, her head hung low.

"I wasn't happy," she murmured.

"What?" Sarah asked softly.

"I said I wasn't happy. I saw things, too, but even though we saw the same things, we saw them differently. Clay did have his new friend, and his new dog, but you had a new friend, too... Daniel.

"It seemed like every time I went looking for you, you were with him, or Grandma, and were always doing something with them. Papa Joe and Pa were always working, and then Lillian came along and well... I felt left out. I didn't feel like I fit in anymore."

Mary wiped angrily at the tears in her eyes. She started to get up, but Sarah reached out for her.

"Mary, I'm so sorry. You're absolutely right. It used to be just you and me, and since I found this book, it's been just me and my thoughts. Please, don't be mad. I'm so, so sorry.

"Please stay. There's more that I haven't told you, and this secret will be between you, me, and Clay. You must pinky swear that you will not tell a soul. Do you swear?"

"I promise I'll never tell a soul until you tell me I can. Remember, I'm not a baby now and I'm gonna prove it. You can trust me, I swear." Clay solemnly looked at his sisters, kissed his little finger and stuck it out toward them.

Mary and Sarah followed his lead, kissed their fingers and interlocked them with his. "We swear," they said in unison.

"Come with me. Hurry," Sarah said in a whisper. She rose and motioned for them to follow.

Peeking out the door and seeing no one around, Sarah placed her fingers to her lips, and they tiptoed as fast as they could up the stairs to the second floor. Mary and Clay looked at each other in surprise when Sarah hurried past her room and went to the end of the hallway. Stopping in front of what looked like a wide closet door, their sister smiled slyly, reached in her pocket, and pulled out a key.

"What's that?" Mary asked, staring at the object in her sister's hand.

Mary wrapped her arms tightly around herself, and scrunched her shoulders up to her ears. Sticking a finger in her mouth, she bit her nail, and peered over her shoulder, as if someone might sneak up on them.

"Shh," Sarah whispered, and placed her fingers to her lips again. "Our secret, remember?"

Clay beamed and Mary nodded, although she frowned, and looked nervously over her shoulder again.

"Shouldn't we at least tell Grandma or Lillian?" Mary asked, chewing on her lower lip.

"Lillian must concentrate on her health, and Grandma must concentrate on Lillian, as well as all of us. We don't want either one of them worrying about anything else right now, do we? We must make life as calm and comfortable for them as we can. We can tell everyone about this later, when all the excitement is over and the baby is here, fair enough?"

Mary nodded, but didn't look too convinced.

Sarah paused and looked at her sister tenderly. "Mary, you're a good and gentle person, and it
worries you to see anyone in trouble. But you need
some adventure in your life. You need to do something daring and different. What we are about to do
isn't dangerous, and we aren't breaking any rules.
This is an adventure, an experience that we may
never have again. If you don't want to go with us,
I'll understand, but you must keep our secret. What
do you want to do?"

Mary listened to Sarah, chewed on her lip
again, and wrinkled her nose. After a short time, she
took a deep breath and looked at Clay and Sarah.

"Let's go. You're right. I'm a goody two-shoes
and it's boring. As long as we're not going to get into
trouble, and we're not doing anything wrong, I'm
willing to give it a try."

She nodded firmly and watched as Sarah
smiled, inserted the key into the door lock, twisted
until it clicked, and turned the knob. She pulled the
door open, and Clay clutched Mary's hand. They
peered into the doorway that revealed a dusty staircase, crisscrossed with cobwebs that led into a black
void.

~ ELEVEN ~
Sarah Shares Her Secret

Daniel spent the rest of the day in his new room. Each time he struggled to stand up right, he found his legs weak and rubbery, and his arms felt heavy, as if he were holding full buckets of water. Working his tongue in and out of his mouth, it felt thick and fuzzy, and his senses swam from fantasy to reality.

Irene and Lillian hovered over him, placing cool cloths on his forehead, feeding him broth and tea.

Slowly, minute by minute, the blurry pictures in his mind melded together, and Daniel was able to focus his thoughts. The fur dissolved from his tongue, enabling him to finally speak. Daniel took a deep breath, and blinked hard.

"Thank you so much. I-I don't know what happened, but I feel better now. I-I really do," he mumbled weakly.

"I'm going to draw the curtains and darken the room. Try to get some sleep, and give your body a chance to return to normal," Lillian said.

Irene smoothed the quilt, and replaced the warm cloth on his forehead with a cool one. The women tiptoed from the room, closed the door, leaving him to rest.

Daniel's mind raced, examining what he just heard. Everything he knew, or thought he knew, was a lie. Not just a lie, but a blatant insult to him and to the woman his grandfather had betrayed.

Daniel rubbed his head roughly, and threw back the covers. Stumbling to the window, he stared out across the yard, past the gardens to the meadow beyond. All his life he had been hard, unfeeling, angry, and aching for revenge.

Revenge for his father and grandfather, and for the life he had always been told was taken from him. But now he didn't feel hard or uncaring. He felt small, vulnerable, and exposed.

The Wilkins' had opened up their home to him. Clay had accepted him as a surrogate brother, and now Sarah had revealed her closest secret to him. They had all trusted him, and he had done nothing but plan to deceive and rob them.

Tears came to his eyes when he realized what he had turned into—his grandfather, a cold, harsh, unloving creature with nothing on his mind but taking from others, tricking, lying and betraying them.

He also cried for his father, who felt he had failed as a son and a father. His father, who fell in love, lost his wife in death, and then turned to drink and opium dens to drown out the sound of insults and criticism.

His last words to Daniel, as he lay dying were, "Son, I'm sorry I failed you."

Daniel thought then that he was apologizing for failing to find the trail to the gold, but now he knew he was wrong. His father was apologizing for not saving him from his grandfather.

"It's all right, Papa," he had sobbed. "It's not too late for me. You did the best you could.'"

Daniel wiped his eyes and washed his face with the damp cloth. He was truly exhausted now. Collapsing back onto the bed, he closed his eyes, and fell into a restless asleep.

Upstairs, events were unfolding that would solve his problems, and change his life forever.

~ * ~

Sarah, Mary, and Clay crept up the stairs to the dark void of the attic, cringing and swatting at dusty cobwebs that swayed toward them, and clung to their hair and clothes. Reaching the top step, the trio emerged through the dark opening to the highest floor. Sarah paused and lit a lamp she had placed there earlier on a nearby table. Going to the nearby window, she pulled the heavy curtain to one side, and light oozed into the dark, gloomy room through the grimy pane.

When all the curtains were opened, Mary blew out the lamp, and she and Clay stared at the many pieces of old furniture and crates stacked around.

"Wow, there sure is a lot of junk up here," Clay said. "Sarah, can I look around, is it alright?"

"Sure," Sarah answered.

She knew just how he felt. She had been as curious as he was the first time she came up here.

"You two look around, just be careful and don't break anything. And while you're looking, listen as I read something I found in Aimee's book."

"Who's book?" Mary stopped suddenly and looked at her sister.

Sarah smiled sheepishly. "I forgot to tell you. I was reading this book to Daniel when he got sick. Let me tell you what I discovered."

Sarah retold Clay Jr. and Mary the story she had read to Daniel. The children sat looking amazed and shocked when she finished.

"I can't believe she went through that much pain and heartache over that horrid man," Mary cried.

"I know. Think of being on a ship in that storm

for days. She could have been killed. And she had to watch all those people drown. It must have been horrible, just horrible," Sarah added.

"But the gold," Clay said, staring out the window. "Think about all that gold she got."

"That's why we're here," Sarah said with a smile. "Listen."

Sarah sat by the window and thumbed through the journal. She finally found the page she searched for and began to read.

> *They say that money doesn't buy you happiness, and while that may be true in most cases, I must say that it can give you independence, security, and the ability to help others. I have had the good fortune to be able to live quite nicely on the returns from my investments in John Deere and Atlantic Telegraph Company.*
>
> *I have, therefore, the bulk of the gold still in my possession. Regardless of the circumstances surrounding my acquiring the gold, I still have nightmares of that fateful day aboard the Central America. I can recall to this day, the fear and terror on the faces of the passengers and crew, who were still on board when my lifeboat pulled away that last time, just hours before all was lost.*
>
> *Although I realize their blood is not on my hands, I feel I must do something in their name to make their deaths not in vain. And that Abram Ginsberg's gift to me would not only bring me security and comfort, but do the same for the many generations that will follow. I have therefore devised this plan.*

I will pass on the gold to those who come along after me. In our early life we all have dreams of how we want to spend our tomorrows. We imagine the perfect job, the perfect love, the perfect family, peace, happiness and comfort for our loved ones for all of our days, but they are just that... dreams.

The perfect job I cannot provide, the perfect love, I'm not one to comment on that, the perfect family, I can only see in visions, and peace, that is within one's heart, happiness is a state of mind, but comfort... now, that's where I come in. These other things cannot be bought, but comfort is available for sale.

My history with the child, Isaac, and the game we played, gave me thought as to how to pass my treasure on to whoever is reading this book. I will provide a way for a deserving man, woman, or family to gain possession of this house, and in turn, a future for them to pass on to their family and another deserving person.

This gift, this treasure must live on for centuries. This treasure now belongs to you. All you have to do is find it. It is a prize you must earn. I will leave you a beginning clue, and each clue will lead you to another and another. In the end, if you solve the clues, you will reap the reward of your hard work— the treasure of Abram Ginsberg, the gold that was saved from the sinking S. S. Central America. Good luck. Here is your first clue:

The Gold was found in moun-

Bobbie Shafer

*tains high, and in icy foothill
streams
And you must look high and low
To fulfill your wildest dreams.
To search for hidden treasure
You must look at every clue,
It isn't where the eagle flies
But where the eagle flew.*

"What does she mean, Sarah?" Mary threw up her hands, and cocked her head.

"What does it mean?" Clay squealed. "It means we're rich, rich, rich." He jumped up and started leaping around.

"Not so fast, Clay," Sarah said. "We have to solve the clues first, and I've got a feeling it's not going to be easy. Do you know what that clue means?"

"Read it again," Clay said, squatting down before her.

Sarah read the short poem again, this time slowly, emphasizing each word.

"Not where the eagle flies," Mary said thoughtfully, "but where it flew."

"Look high and low," Clay murmured.

"I thought we'd start high," Sarah suggested, "and this is the highest place I could think of."

"Good idea," Clay cried. He leaped to his feet and began looking around. "Can we take the sheets off the furniture?"

"I guess so, as long as we put everything back like it was," Sarah replied.

"Sarah?" Mary said softly. "Are we going to tell Lillian and Pa about the treasure?"

Sarah gathered up the sheet she had just removed from a chair and sat down.

"I've been thinking about that." She looked down, and then back at her brother and sister. "I don't think so. I may not be the only one to have read this. What if someone else has already found the gold? They'll just think we're silly for believing this journal. If we get stumped on one of the clues... well, maybe we'll tell them then, but for now, let's just look ourselves."

"Can we tell Daniel? He won't think we're silly," Clay said. "He could help, I know he would."

"Let's think about it a while. Later, we'll talk about it again. Let's just look around for a while, okay? Let it be our secret for a while."

Clay nodded and resumed his search.

"Ooh, did you feel that cold breeze?" Mary asked, and rubbed her hands across her chill-bumped arms.

"It is cold up here, silly," Clay quipped.

"I know *that*. I mean the wind that just blew across me. Is there a window open?"

She walked to the front wall and checked the windows.

"There's none open. I just drew back the drapes when we came in. I would have noticed if a window was broken or open," Sarah said.

"Didn't you feel it?" Mary hugged herself tightly.

Clay didn't answer but shook his head, and Sarah grunted, "Uh-uh."

Mary continued to walk around, searching the ceiling for a hole or crack where the breeze came in. When she reached the spot she had been before, she gasped.

"Come over here, hurry."

Sarah and Clay joined her, and she pulled them near her. "Do you feel it now?"

"Gosh, she's right, Sarah. It's much colder here. Look, you can even see her skirt moving."

Clay frowned and moved his hand back and forth in the coolness.

Sarah stood and let the icy air flow over her. She closed her eyes and her arms dropped to her sides. Mary and Clay stepped back and watched their sister go into a trance-like state. She breathed normally, and her color was the same, but she seemed to be asleep.

"Sarah?" Clay whispered in alarm.

"Shh," Mary cautioned. "Wait a minute and see what happens."

A slight smile played along Sarah's mouth, and she appeared to be dreaming.

Clay could stand it no longer. "Sarah? Sarah, are you alright?" He reached over and jerked at his sister's sleeve.

Sarah's eyes few open, and she worked her lips a few times before she could speak.

"She's here. She's always been here," she cried.

"She who?" Clay gasped, and looked from one side to the other.

"Aimee. Aimee McKay. She's still here at Eagle Creek."

Sarah squatted, and began shoving crates back, grabbing at small boxes. Dust began to fly and Mary began sneezing. When she finished, she saw Sarah frantically pulling on a small trunk, which seemed to be stuck between two crates.

"Sarah, let me help." Mary said, grabbing her sister around her waist.

She tugged hard at her sister, and when Sarah finally let go, she fell back, and Mary pushed one of the crates to the side, and the chest slid forward easily.

"Is it locked?" Sarah asked anxiously.

"I don't think so but it has two fasteners," Mary said. "You knew it was here, so you open it."

She moved over, and Clay huddled next to her, peering curiously over her shoulder.

"Sister?" Clay said softly. "How *did* you know it was here?"

"*She* told me," Sarah said dreamily. "Aimee told me."

Sarah reached for the golden latches, and unfastened them. She moved so slowly it was as if she was still in the trance.

With the dreamy smile still on her face, Sarah paused after lifting the hinges of the lock. She gazed at the chest, and then tenderly raised the lid.

There was a layer of thin, pale blue paper over a shallow tray on top. Sarah slid her hands under the paper, and carefully shifted it to the top of a nearby box. The velvet lined tray was divided into several compartments. Two of the sections cradled two small lockets. One on a delicate gold chain, and the other was a delicate cameo on a tiny silver ribbon. A man's pocket watch nestled in a small partition. There were cuff links, watch fobs, watch chains, and gold button studs for dress shirts.

Sarah moved a wad of cotton from a corner section. A small black, velvet box sat in the back. With trembling hands, Sarah opened the lid. The siblings' gasps echoed in the vastness. A large gold ring, set with what looked like dozens of sparkling diamonds, sat in a thin slot cut into the bottom of the box.

"Shall I call P-Pa?" Clay whispered.

"No," Sarah said. "Let's see what else is in here."

She curled her fingers into the openings on either side of the tray, lifted it gently, and handed it to Mary, who set it on a crate beside her.

Another paper was removed, revealing a soft shimmering cloth, folded neatly across the top.

"O-o-o-h," Mary cooed, and reached over to stroke it.

Sarah held part of it up, and they all tenderly touched the hundreds of tiny pearls sewn across the bodice of the shimmering dress. Sarah wrapped the paper back around the dress, moved it to the side, and looked down.

There were books with well-worn covers, and small, tin pictures of stiff looking subjects standing frozen in time. Some of them were of the Washingtons, and some were of people they didn't recognize. At the bottom was a photograph of a short, slim, well-dressed man, standing with one hand in his pocket, and the other resting on a chest. He wore a suit, coat, and a hat pulled down low on his forehead.

"That's her," Sarah whispered softly. "That's Aimee."

"How do you know?" Clay asked.

"Look how tiny she is. See how thick the soles of her shoes are? She's trying to look taller. Even with layers of clothes, she couldn't hide how tiny she was. Notice how delicate her features are, and her fingers are long and thin. She wrote that she fooled everyone but Isaac's mother, Rose, who knew Mack Kaymey was a woman. I'm sure, in time, they all knew. After all, she saved their lives. They would never betray her," Sarah said reverently.

"Who's this?" Mary asked.

She held up a picture of the same well-dressed, small man, with another figure standing close. One man was tall, blond and handsome. One arm rested across the smaller man's shoulders, while his other arm was bent to the side, his thumb hooked in his pocket.

"That must be Lucas. That's the man who was on the ship with her. He moved here to Sycamore Grove and built a house on the property next to hers. They fell in love and got married."

"What's that?" Clay asked, and pointed to a shiny box in the bottom corner.

Sarah pulled it out and lifted the lid.

Nestled in the box was an enormous gold nugget. The size took their breath away.

"Sarah," Clay begged. "Can I hold it, please?"

Sarah handed him the small box, and Clay dumped it into his hand.

"Is this it?" he asked. "Is this the treasure?" He turned the nugget over and over in his hand.

"Is it?" Mary echoed, her face mirroring Clays.

Sarah smiled and shook her head. "I don't think so. I think this is a souvenir, you know, a keepsake from her experience on the sinking ship."

"We have to tell Pa and Lillian," Mary insisted.

Sarah looked at both of them. Clay nodded, still clutching the egg-size nugget.

Mary grabbed Sarah's arm. "Sister, Papa spent all he had to buy this place. They are working themselves to the bone trying to provide a living for us.

"Lillian and Grandma are up from dawn to

dark hoeing, planting, harvesting, and canning so we'll have food this winter, and it just isn't fair to let this sit here because it's a dead woman's souvenir."

"They're all downstairs in the kitchen," Clay said. "We can take it to them now, and you must tell them what you know. Sarah, this isn't a game, it's our life."

Sarah gaped at her siblings' grown-up attitudes and speech.

Finally she nodded. "You're right. This isn't just a piece of fiction I'm reading. I forgot for a while that this *is* real. Let's go."

Suddenly, the tiny breeze they once felt became a gale. The thin papers from the trunk whirled and flew through the air. Their hair blew straight back, and Mary's dress flew up, almost covering her head.

They covered their faces as dust and sheets danced around the attic, and papers soared like hawks overhead.

"Is she mad?" Mary whimpered. "I didn't mean to make her mad."

She began to sob, and as soon as she began to cry, the melee stopped. Mary felt a gentle touch across her cheek.

Sarah straightened up and glanced around. "No, Mary, I think she's happy. I don't think she meant to frighten you. She was just expressing her joy the only way she could."

~ TWELVE ~
Words From Beyond

The family looked stunned while Sarah read Aimee's journal to them in the kitchen. The only sound was the occasional clink as someone placed their coffee cup back on a saucer.

When she was finished, she nodded to Clay who went to their father, placed the box on the table, and, with his mouth working to suppress a smile, slowly lifted the lid, exposing the nugget.

Irene gasped, and jerked her apron to her mouth. Lillian's face went slack, and Sarah thought for a moment she was going to faint, until she finally took another deep breath.

Joseph shot out of his chair, knocking it backwards. He adjusted his glasses, and stared at the golden rock.

"Clayton, is it real gold?" Joseph's voice sounded hoarse with emotion.

Clayton shook his head and shrugged. "I'm not an expert, but it feels like gold."

He held the nugget, raising his hand up and down, trying to estimate its weight. He picked up a knife and pressed the edge into the metal.

"It's soft, and it's the right color. It feels right." He slowly smiled, and looked from one face to another.

"Papa, how much money do you think that gold is worth?" Clay asked, looking hopefully at his father.

"Well," he grinned, "this here little rock is worth more than I made in several years working six days a week at the cotton mill."

"Wow," Clay said, sounding awestruck. "Papa, if there *is* a treasure, you and Lillian, and Papa Joe and Grandma, will never, ever have to work a day in your life again."

Clayton laughed nervously. "Before we start putting our feet up, let's take this to the assayer and make sure it's what we think it is."

"Can we go, Pa? Can we?" Clay cried. "Sarah found the chest, Mary helped get it out, and I saw the box it was in. Can we all go?"

Lillian still seemed to be in shock, but nodded numbly when they looked at her for permission.

"Are you sure it's safe to leave you, hon?" Clayton asked, looking troubled.

"I don't think this baby is in any hurry," Irene remarked with a smile. "It'll be a couple of weeks, I'm sure."

"I'll stay with the women," Joseph volunteered.

"I'd feel better if you were with us," Clayton said. "You can read people better than I can. I want to be sure I'm getting an honest assay."

"You go ahead, Joseph," Lillian finally spoke. "I feel fine. Irene will be here if I need her."

"If you ladies are sure," Joseph said, hesitantly.

"And what good are you men when the time comes, anyhow?" Irene grinned. "You'd just walk up and down the hallway, the way you did when the other young'uns came along."

"We'll go first thing in the morning," Clayton said. "Yes, you children can come along."

~ * ~

As the children whooped and hollered, Daniel backed away from his door at the kitchen. He had been standing with his ear pressed against the wooden panel, and heard every word.

When Sarah read to him Aimee's version of her past, the guilt of following his grandfather's plan had overwhelmed him, but now greed was rearing its ugly head. Had Aimee stayed with Marcus, had not given up on him during his weak moments, perhaps he would have been successful in winning a fortune from the miners. In a way, the gold was rightfully his.

Daniel shook his head and rubbed his face. He was confused, where did those thoughts come from? He didn't want to rob these people who had opened their hearts and home to him. But what right did they have to the gold?

They hadn't tracked Aimee's journey from California to South Carolina like his grandfather had. None of them had seen the newspapers announcing the loss of the S.S. South America, and realized that she had not been listed as a survivor, although everyone remembered her being lowered into the lifeboat. It was Marcus who figured out that she had escaped with a small fortune in gold from the sinking ship, wasn't it?

Daniel almost screamed for the voice in his head to shut up. His heart raced, his palms sweat, a tic developed at the corner of his eye, the same type of tic his grandfather had. What was happening to him? What was going on? How could his grandfather's thoughts be forcing themselves into his head? Was he losing his mind?

Climbing back into bed, he began to feel the room sway. He closed his eyes, and a cool breath of air caressed his forehead and cheeks. He slipped into a restless sleep, while the hint of a soft lullaby drifted in from far away, nearly inaudible.

~ * ~

The next morning, Clayton, Joseph, and the children pulled away from the house just as the sun peeped over the hill.

Irene and Lillian finished the breakfast dishes and Irene wiped the table down. Daniel finished eating with the family, and poured them all a cup of tea, when someone suddenly banged on the back door. Daniel held up his hand to the ladies and motioned them back. He picked up a large kitchen knife and hid it behind his leg, then jerked the door open.

Albert Washington stood on the porch, gasping for breath. His eyes bulged, and his mouth opened and closed as he struggled for words.

"Albert?" Lillian cried, when she saw his distress. "What's wrong?"

She and Irene rushed forward, as Daniel stepped back out of the way. Lillian pulled Albert in from the cold and rubbed his icy hands.

"Ma... Ma wanted..." tears filled his eyes.

"Albert, calm down," Irene said in a soothing voice. "Take a deep breath and speak slowly.

"It's my sister, Miss Irene. She's in a bad way. It's the baby. Her time came night before last, but something's wrong. The baby... May... Please come, Miss Irene. Miss Lillian, Ma needs help. My sister needs your help." By now, tears flowed freely down Albert's face.

"Lillian, will you fix a pot of hot chocolate for our young friend here? You are not going, so don't even start. Albert, it won't take me five minutes to grab a few things and be on my way. Daniel, saddle a horse for me."

After snapping out instructions, Irene grabbed her coat, a small bag and began stuffing it with jars from the cabinet.

Daniel ran at full speed to the barn, and had the disgruntled horse saddled in no time. He had just finished when Irene arrived, and with a boost up, she was on her way to the Washington home.

By the time Daniel returned to the kitchen, Albert had relaxed somewhat, and was telling Lillian all about May. She was his favorite sister, and was one of the oldest. May was the motherly type. She spent hours tending to all the younger children, reading, playing, bathing them, and taking them on picnics.

When May and George announced their desire to marry, it was no surprise since they had been best friends all their lives. This was their first child, and they had been happy and excited but now, everyone was frightened and worried.

Lillian went to Albert. "I know you're worried about your sister, but I can assure you, Irene has de-livered dozens of babies, and knows exactly what to do."

"She does? Is you sure?" Albert chewed on his fingernail.

"Oh yes, I'm very sure. Irene delivered Clay's mother, she delivered Sarah, Mary, and Clay. People all over the county used to call on her when the womenfolk were about to deliver." Lillian cupped Albert's chin in her hand.

"Really?" Albert took a deep breath.

"Really. I know this because when she found out our baby was on the way, she wanted me to know I had nothing to worry about—and I'm not wor-ried at all."

Daniel sat at the table and watched the interaction between Lillian and Albert. He remembered his dying when he was too young to really remember her. He felt cheated and sad that there had never been anyone tender and gentle in his life. All he remembered was being left alone, preached to, and having it hammered into him over and over about the injustice of the outcome of his grandfather and Aimee McKay's relationship. He wasn't taught love, loyalty, friendship, or compassion. He was taught vengeance, retribution, and pay back.

Suddenly in the middle of Lillian's conversation, she stiffened and gasped. Looking startled and confused, she took a deep breath, smiled, and nodded.

"Are you all right?" Daniel asked, coming out of his reverie.

"Oh, yes, it's nothing, I'm sure. Don't be concerned." She rose slowly, clutching her enlarged stomach, and placed a plate of raisin bread on the table.

"Albert, you must eat something. I'm sure you haven't eaten a bite in... o-o-o-o-h!" She bent over and grabbed the table for balance.

"Lillian?" Daniel cried, wringing his hands. "What can I do?"

"Can... can you h-h-elp me to Irene's room? I think I'd better lie down." A fine sheen of perspiration now glowed on her forehead and upper lip.

Daniel grabbed her arm, and helped her to the bedroom. He felt her squeeze his hand hard, and heard her gasp again. She was now bent over farther, and stumbled.

She threw her head back and closed her eyes. "Hurry, Daniel, hurry. The baby's coming. You've got to help me."

"Oh, tarnation, Lillian, let me go after Irene. I don't have a clue what to do," Daniel said, sounding panicky.

"Don't leave me, Daniel, please. I need you here. May's family needs Irene now. This baby is her first and she's in trouble. I don't think there'll be any problems here.

"Get some clean sheets from the hall closet. Put some water on to boil and wash your hands. Find the scissors in Irene's sewing box and put them in the boiling water. Get some strong twine from the kitchen drawer, cut two pieces about ten inches long, and put them in the water also. I'll need a damp cloth and a wet towel.

"Hurry, Daniel, we don't have much time."

Lillian sat on the edge of the bed, and began to remove her sweater, shoes, and stockings.

As Daniel ran back into the kitchen, he threw a few pieces of wood into the stove to get the fire roaring.

"Scissors, string, hot water," Daniel repeated.

Albert jumped up and handed him a large pot, and Daniel put just enough water to cover the scissors and twine, and set it on the stove. He ran to the hall closet and grabbed two clean sheets. By the time he returned to the kitchen, Albert had put the scissors and twine in the water.

"Hey, Albert," Daniel said, trying to sound happy and cheerful. "Thanks a lot. This is a new experience for me. I need all the help I can get. Is there anything else we need?"

Before Albert could answer, a moan came from the bedroom. There was silence, and then Lillian cried, "I need that wet cloth and towel. Is anyone still there?"

Daniel ran to the door. "I'll get them right away. Here're the sheets. The scissors and twine are in the water. Why are they in water?"

Lillian almost burst out laughing, but a pain hit her, and she sucked in a breath. When it had passed, Daniel was by her side with the damp cloth and towel.

"We boil anything that might be dirty, or have anything on it that might harm the baby. He, or she, must be born in a clean environment."

Lillian placed the towel by her side, and put the cloth in her mouth, between her teeth. She threw the clean sheet over the lower half of her body, and slipped out of her underclothes. Gripping the sheets in her fists, a muffled groan came from between her teeth and the cloth.

The pains were almost constant now, and Daniel paced the room. His thoughts were jumbled and painful. He wanted to comfort Lillian and make everything better. He wanted the pain to go away. Why was she having a baby? Didn't she already take care of three children? What kind of woman would put herself through that much pain for a child? How could everybody just go off and leave her alone at this time?

"Sis-s-a," she mumbled. "Sis-s-s-a," she said again.

Daniel rushed to her side. "What? What are you saying?"

"A-a-a-a-a-h," she screamed, and held up her hand, working two fingers together, opening and closing them.

"Scissors," Daniel cried and rushed to the kitchen.

He tore through the drawers until he found a long metal fork. He snatched up the fork and used it to hook the scissors, and lifted them from the steaming water.

"Clean cloth," he yelled at Albert. "I need a clean cloth."

"I-e-e-e-a." Another cry came from the bedroom.

Albert ran into the hall and came back with a pillow case.

Daniel placed the hot scissors and the pieces of twine on the pillow case, and carefully carried them into the bedroom.

As he entered the bedroom he glanced up, and almost dropped the pillow case. Lillian was bent over, picking up a tiny, wriggling, wet object. She turned it over, and slapped it's wrinkled behind. She slapped it again, and the baby produced an ear-splitting wail from its screwed up little face.

Lillian's hair was dripping wet, and her face was covered with perspiration, but she was glowing with happiness.

"Bring them here," she said with a smile, and motioned for him to come closer.

She tied the string in two places and picked up the scissors. With a precise and steady hand, she cut the umbilical cord between the two strings. Lillian took the wet towel and bathed the baby from head to toe, and wrapped it in a sheet. Leaning back on the pillow, Lillian suddenly jerked upright again.

"Oh, my," she whispered. "Daniel," she moaned. "Take the baby. I think there's another one."

"What?" Daniel screamed. "What another one? *Another one?*"

Daniel ran to the chest and pulled out a drawer. Placing the baby inside, he hurried back to Lillian.

"More cord," she groaned. "Boil the scissors again." She collapsed back onto the bed.

Daniel grabbed the scissors from her, and ran to the kitchen. "Get ready, again," he shouted at Albert. "There's another one coming."

He cut two more pieces of string, and dropped the scissors and sections of string into the pot, then tapped his foot impatiently.

He heard moans, groans, and muffled cries coming from the bedroom.

Albert brought another wet towel and stood with Daniel, watching the water bubble around the scissors.

When Daniel heard the final scream, followed by another series of slaps from the bedroom, and the wail of a second child, he fished the scissors and twine from the pot. He placed the items on the sheet Albert gave him, and raced back to the bedroom.

Lillian looked as if she had just defeated an entire tribe of scalp-hunting savages. And yet her smile, and the look in her eyes, made Daniel feel whole, complete... as if this was what life was all about.

"Mercy," the new mother gasped with a sigh. "This was certainly unexpected."

After cutting the second cord, cleaning and wrapping the second baby, she looked embarrassed.

"Is there anything else I can do?" Daniel stood limply by her bed.

"I hate to ask you, but if you could strip down the bed, bring some clean sheets, and a clean gown from my room, I'd really appreciate it." She smiled shyly.

"Is that all?" He laughed. "I can do that without any help. Well, maybe I'll ask Albert to help. He's dying to do something."

"Thank you. Could you bring my other baby to me first?" She murmured, leaned back and closed her eyes.

Daniel brought the first baby to her, then stood by and watched Lillian stroke their silky cheeks, and examine each tiny finger. He noticed their little mouths open and close, and their little arms reach wildly in the air. His heart softened, his life changed, his world became brand new.

Daniel grew.

Within the hour, the bed was changed, and Lillian was clean, wearing a fresh gown. The babies had been examined and cleaned again, and her new son and daughter nestled next to their mother, who had fallen fast asleep.

She reminded Daniel of a painting he'd seen in New Orleans. It had been Christmastime in a church that he had seen a picture of a woman and her baby, called *God's Gift to Us*.

Here it was nearly Christmas again, and surely these two little babies would be the best gift of all.

~ THIRTEEN ~
Unexpected Gifts

Daniel and Albert heated more water, washed the linens, and while they were hanging them up, Irene rode into the yard.

"How is May?" Albert yelled, when she stopped.

"May is just fine. You're an uncle now, Albert. She had a little girl. The little darling wanted to come out feet first, but I got her turned around in time."

She seemed to notice for the first time that the men were standing in the cold winter wind, hanging up clothes.

"Daniel, what in the world are you two doing? It isn't washday. If that Lillian took it upon herself to wash clothes..." Irene swung her leg over the saddle horn and slid into Daniel's waiting arms, as he helped her down.

Daniel and Albert grinned at one another as Albert continued to hang up the sheets.

"Young man, this isn't one bit funny. I told her..."

"She didn't wash, Miss Irene. We did," Albert laughed, jabbing Daniel with his elbow.

"Why in Heaven's name would you do that?" She demanded, unknotting her wool scarf and pulling off her gloves.

"We didn't want the dirty sheets in the house with the babies," Daniel mumbled, and went back to helping Albert.

"Our sheets weren't dirty enough to hurt the ba..." Irene froze as Daniel's words sank in.

"Lillian," she cried, and flew across the yard,

into the house, her gloves and scarf falling to the ground.

"She's in your room," Daniel called after her, and both he and Albert burst into laughter.

"I'd better git home," Albert said. "I want to see May and my new niece."

"Thanks for all your help, Albert. I couldn't have done it without you," Daniel said sincerely, giving the boy a tight hug.

"If I couldn't help May, at least I could help Miss Lillian," Albert said, beaming. "Tell Clay I'll see him later."

"I will. They should be home soon. Aren't they in for a surprise?"

After checking on Lillian and making sure she and the babies were all healthy and comfortable, Irene went into the kitchen and began to cut up roast from the day before to make a big pot of stew.

Daniel unsaddled Irene's horse, rubbed him down, and brought him grain and water. He fed the chickens, brought in the eggs, pitched hay to the cattle, and milked old Sukey. Carrying the milk into the kitchen, he poured some into the churn, and the rest into a large metal pitcher.

It was almost two o'clock when Clayton pulled the wagon to a stop by the barn.

He and Joseph unhitched the team while Sarah, Mary, and Clay grabbed packages from the wagon bed and ran to the house.

"Lillian, wait till you see what we bought for the baby," Sarah called out.

They piled packages on the table and rushed to the fire to warm their numb fingers.

"Yeah, Grandma, and wait till you see what Papa Joe bought you," Clay piped in.

"Hush, Clay," Mary snapped. "That's for him to tell, not you."

"We got something for Daniel, too," Clay whispered with a grin.

"Me? I don't need a single thing," Daniel argued, as he stepped from his room into the kitchen.

Joseph and Clayton stomped their feet and came in the back door, laughing and slapping each other on the back.

"Look outside, young'uns, it's starting to snow. You better get your chores done before it gets any worse," their father advised.

"No need, sir," Daniel said. "They're all done. I even stacked up wood by the back, plenty by the stove, and I filled up the wood box by the fireplace. No need to get anymore today."

Joseph grinned and nodded to Clayton. "Well, boy, I guess you'll be happy to learn that it's payday."

"It's what?" Daniel asked.

"Tell 'em Papa. Tell 'em 'bout the gold," Clay urged, dancing all around.

"Oh, the nugget," Irene said. "I'd forgotten all about that."

Joseph's mouth dropped open, and Clayton gave her a shocked look.

"Forgot? Forgot? How in tarnation could you forget about a gold nugget?" Joseph asked in disbelief.

"You watch your mouth, old man," Irene growled. "You have no idea what went on around here after you all left. First, Albert came tearing in here saying his sister was dying in childbirth. I rushed to their house, and after almost losing the child, helped her deliver a beautiful baby girl.

"Second, while I was gone, and you all were in town fiddle-faddling around over a chunk of gold, Lillian went into labor, and Daniel and Albert helped her deliver not one, but *two* babies," she paused, gasping for breath, her eyes blazing. "Now don't you raise your voice to me about my memory."

"Oh, gracious, gracious," Joseph wheezed, as his breath left him.

"Where is she?" Clayton asked.

Irene pointed toward her bedroom, turned her back on Joseph, and went back to the stove to stir the stew.

"Is she okay?" Joseph whispered, coming up behind his wife.

"She's fine," she answered sharply, "thanks to Daniel and Albert."

"Daniel, my boy, you saved little Clay, and now you've saved my daughter-in-law and—did you say two babies?" He stopped and gazed blankly at Daniel.

Daniel grinned and nodded. "Yes, sir, twins, a boy and a girl, but I did very little, sir. It was all Miss Lillian, she did it all. She's a real brave lady, she is. I didn't save anybody, mostly just paced, like Miss Irene said earlier."

"You were here, and she told me everything you did. She couldn't have done it alone, Daniel, and that's the truth. I know how hard that must have been for you, and we'll be forever grateful," Irene said softly.

Clayton came in, smiling in wonder. "They're beautiful, just beautiful. We're naming one Joseph Albert, and the other Daniela Roberta. I hope you don't mind, Daniel?"

Tears burned his eyes. He quickly went to the table and slid heavily into a chair, covering his face with both hands.

"Please, sit down. I have something to tell you," Daniel mumbled through his fingers. "And, if after I'm finished, you want me to leave, I'll pack my bags and be gone today."

"What are you talking about?" Sarah asked.

"I don't know how to begin, so I'll just start. My first memory is my grandfather, Marcus Alexander. Yes, Sarah, that name is familiar, and it should be. He was the same Marcus Alexander that seduced and lured Aimee McKay away from her father to the gold fields in California.

"Apparently he planned to cheat all the gold miners out of their gold, and used Aimee's inheritance to do it, except it backfired and he lost everything. He became a bitter, cruel, and black-hearted old man, who, when he realized his son would not, or could not, keep up the search for Aimee, turned his venomous ways on me, a young, gullible child.

"My grandfather became obsessed with Aimee and swore to find her after he saw her leave on the S.S. Sonora. When she wasn't among those rescued in South Carolina, he began to speculate that she had not only survived, but was the woman seen on the deck before the women were placed in the lifeboats. The rumors died out but my grandfather was fanatical about finding her and the gold.

"His search led him to Charleston, and I was by his side as he combed through courthouse records, trying to pick up the slightest clue to her whereabouts. He found her but was arrested and sent back to California for crimes I didn't even know about.

"Grandfather escaped, and drove my father to his death, but I was caught up in his fantasy. I found records of land purchases that led me here. I felt sure this was the place. When Sarah found the journal, I knew it was just a matter of time until I found the gold that I was convinced belonged to me, and was my rightful inheritance.

"But I met you all, and day after day, week after week, month after month, I saw a life that I didn't believe existed. A life filled with love, compassion, sacrifice, and happiness. Meeting people who were forgiving and nonjudgmental was new to me. I've never known the kindness and caring you show to others, and slowly became confused and bewildered.

"Then, I was blessed today. Today, a woman ignored the pain that a man could never endure, a woman who closed her mind and body to physical torture, and smiled at the experience of bringing precious life into this world.

"My grandfather's voice doesn't haunt me anymore. Pa's desolate face doesn't fill my nightmares any longer. Before me now, I see life, opportunities, adventure, chances, and a new beginning.

"The gold doesn't matter to me anymore, except to help you find it for your family. You may scoff at me, but it is obvious Aimee wants you to find it. I believe she has been instrumental in Sarah coming across the book, leading her into the attic, and, believe me, she has warned me to mend my ways.

"I'll leave if you want me to, but I want to stay, help work this farm, rescue the boy inside of me that never had a chance to know happiness, and give him a new future, a new tomorrow. I beg you to forgive me." He bowed his head, and tears trickled down his cheeks.

The only sound was the tick-tock of the grandfather clock in the hall. Sarah cried, while Irene looked at Clayton and Joseph with tears gathering.

Clayton rose, scraping his chair across the floor, and went to the stove. He reached into the cabinet, pulled out several cups and filled them with coffee. He placed a cup in front of Irene and Joseph, and placed the last one in front of Daniel.

"Daniel, I have a few questions, do you mind?" Clayton's voice was low and solemn.

Daniel shook his head, barely looking up.

"Just exactly how old are you?" He sat in the chair next to Daniel, and leaned on the table.

"I'll be eighteen soon, sir. I'll turn eighteen in a couple of months."

"Seventeen?" Joseph's face looked like an approaching storm. "Just seventeen, mercy, boy, how long have you been on your on?"

"My Pa died a few months before my grandpa, and just before my fourteenth birthday. I had just turned fifteen when I got all my Pa's things sold so I'd have enough money to travel. It didn't last long, and I've been working along at different places wherever I traveled. I guess, well, it's been nearly three years now."

"Excuse me." A weak voice came from the doorway.

When they turned, Lillian stood leaning against the frame.

"Lillian, what are you thinking?" Irene cried loudly.

Clayton leaped from the table and rushed to Lillian's side. "You must go back to bed. Why didn't you call us?"

He scooped her into his arms, but she grabbed the door frame to stop him.

"I could make out most of the conversation from the bedroom, but not all. I need to hear this discussion. If you take me back, I'll just get up again."

Clayton looked around wildly for support.

"Let's all go into the living room. Lillian's right, she does have a right to hear this. After what she's been through, she needs to know it all," Irene agreed, smiling at Lillian.

The children rose and started for the living room. Daniel followed, and Joseph, Irene and Clayton, with Lillian in his arms, trailed last.

Clayton laid his wife tenderly on the couch and covered her with a quilt. Joseph added more wood to the fireplace and stirred the coals, while the others made themselves comfortable.

"How old did you say you are, Daniel?" Lillian asked.

"He's not quite eighteen, Lillian," Sarah answered for him. "And everything he led us to believe is a lie," she added curtly.

"Well, you kinda lied, too, Sarah," Clay said defensively.

"I never," she retorted.

"Yeah, you did. You knew all about this Aimee person and you never told us. You knew all about the gold and you kept it to yourself. That's kinda like lying."

"Hush, you two," Irene said, raising her voice.

"Daniel, you have to hear this," Clayton said,

resting his hand on Lillian's ankle.

"I had just moved to Oak Grove, a few miles from Dawson City," he explained. "I had been on my own for about a year after leaving the orphanage at the age of sixteen. No one would hire me because I had no experience, and no family or family friends to recommend me. The only jobs available were back-breaking work laying tracks for the railroad, or sweeping out the local bar.

"I was bitter, broke, and tired of sleeping on the hard floor, or damp ground. I decided that I was going to rob the bank and head for the next state."

"Oh, Clayton, no," Irene cried, and grabbed Joseph's arm.

"Son, I can't believe you're telling us this. That doesn't sound like the man I know," Joseph said gruffly.

"It wasn't me. It was a young man-child who had no direction, had his education beat into him, and had been fed and clothed by people who couldn't get rid of him fast enough. You can't imagine how I felt hearing Daniel talk about love, compassion, and caring. I didn't know about those things, either. I sure hadn't seen much of it in my life.

"I was casing the bank, planning how I was going to carry off the robbery, when the prettiest girl I ever saw came walking down the sidewalk. I could hear her heals snapping on the wooden planks, and she carried her head so high, I could see my future in the reflection of her eyes.

"A ringing started in my ears, and my eyes got blurry. When I re-focused, I saw a tall cowboy walking along side of her, talking to her. He grabbed her arm and tried to get her to stop, but she jerked away and continued walking. He grabbed her again and I forgot all about the bank." Clayton grinned.

"I ran over to that pretty girl, grabbed that yahoo by the throat, and told him if he didn't let her go, I would crush his Adam's apple. I told him that he was manhandling my future wife, and the law wouldn't blame me if I tore him apart."

Lillian smiled. "I wish I could have seen you holding that rude man, defending a girl you hadn't met yet. That's the perfect example of a brave knight."

"I wasn't brave, just mad." Clayton grinned, and his face flushed. "I finally let him go, the man tipped his hat, and apologized while he backed across the street."

"Susan thanked me, introduced herself, and asked what my name was. She said if she was going to marry me, she needed to know what to call me."

"What's this got to do with anything?" Joseph asked harshly.

"It has everything to do with Daniel. Don't you see that sometimes life intervenes with a young man's plans to go down the wrong path? Meeting Susan changed my plans, and meeting all of us changed Daniel's plans."

"The Lord knows what he's doing. Some people aren't smart enough to recognize a second chance when it's shoved in their faces, but the lucky ones do. Clayton was lucky, and so is Daniel. He didn't have to confess all this to us. He did it because he needed to get the poison his grandfather had filled him with, off his chest.

"I've known for some time that Daniel had secrets. I know when my grandchildren have secrets. I know when Clayton has secrets. I also know good people when I see them, and Daniel is good people.

"I have two new grandchildren now, and one of them is named after Daniel. I want him around to see these children grow up. Without Daniel, I'm not sure the twins, or Lillian, would be alive.

"If we're going to have a vote, my vote is for Daniel to become part of this family," Irene said firmly.

~ FOURTEEN ~
Aimee's Gift

Daniel's head reeled from the family meeting. After Irene's speech, everyone began to laugh and agree with her. Clayton had shaken his hand, congratulated him for telling them his story, and Little Clay and Mary told him how happy they were that he was there to help Lillian. Everyone acted as if he had always been a part of their lives.

Daniel smiled, remembering the dressing down Joseph gave him about trying to *put one over on them* as he put it. Joseph told him that he didn't appreciate being duped, and expected everything to be put out front from now on. Then he'd grabbed Daniel's hand, and thanked him again for his part in the birth of the twins. That lecture made him feel as if he was a part of the family

Irene hugged his neck, shook her finger near his nose, and smiled, but Sarah ignored him and acted a little standoffish. He understood her reaction. She had no friends here except those at school plus, living so far out, she didn't see much of them. She had opened her heart, shared her deepest secret with him, only to find out he wasn't who he pretended to be. That stung her pride. It would take some time to win her back, but he had to—he just had to. He'd only just realized how important she was to him.

Clayton finally got around to telling the family the gold nugget the children discovered in the chest was assayed at over five hundred dollars. He gave Daniel thirty-five dollars for his wages from the time his first trial week was over until the present, and then added another thirty-five as a bonus for helping

Lillian deliver the twins.

The family now devoted their time to solving the clue that Sarah found. Although Irene insisted that Lillian stay in bed for at least ten days, Lillian insisted Clayton bring her all the books he could find on eagles.

Joseph took Clay out in the woods looking for abandoned eagles nest, thinking a clue could be there. Daniel and Mary searched through the attic for additional belongings of Aimee's, while Sarah did her chores and pretended she had lost interest.

The household was busy with the twins most of the time. There were always nappies to change, baths to give, and although Lillian was breast feed-ing, one or the other demanded to be held or rocked, when not sleeping. It was rare when they both closed their eyes at the same time.

Soon, Lillian recovered enough to be up and about. She moved slowly but her color was back to normal, and even though she usually had a baby in her arms, she fussed over the other children, and treated them like they were her own.

Snow fell and left a light dusting over the ground. Most of it remained in the shady spots and low areas. Christmas was only a few days away, spurring the family into action. All the women were busy decorating and cooking.

Joseph and Clayton cut a tree, Daniel built a base, and Irene, Lillian, and the children spent an entire evening covering it with paper cut-outs, tin-sel, and tiny candles.

During the past couple of weeks everyone made short, mysterious trips into town. Albert came over a couple of times, once bringing Irene a delicately embroidered scarf handmade by Ruth, to thank her for helping May deliver their first grandchild. On one of the trips into town, Clayton returned with a gift from Elsie Barker.

"I ran into Nat's wife at the store today. She sent you this." Clayton handed the package to Lillian. "That woman's a little strange, if you ask me."

Lillian smiled knowingly while she untied the string, and folded back the wrapping paper.

"Why do you say that?" she asked.

With the paper removed, Lillian saw two sets of tiny crocheted booties, one blue, one pink, and little, knitted-sweaters trimmed to match the booties. She chuckled softly.

"I was about to tell her about the twins, but before I could say anything, she handed me that package and asked how the babies were. How in the world did she know there were two?" Clayton asked.

"You must learn not to ask so many questions, husband. We women are known for our mysterious ways, aren't we?"

His face relaxed and he gazed into Lillian's eyes. Remembering all the hints he felt Susan had sent him, Clayton had to admit, it had been good advice... mysterious, but good. Lillian was right. No more questions.

Clayton bought Albert a tiny wooden pirate's boat for helping Daniel deliver the twins. He hoped that the boat might bring back memories to Isaac about the days he played pirate's treasure with Aimee.

The other gifts were piled under the tree, and everyone enjoyed the scrumptious smells wafting from the kitchen. The tables on the closed-in porch were soon covered with cakes, pies, sweet breads, and several large syrup cakes had been sent from the Washingtons' home for the holidays.

On Christmas Eve, the turkey that Joseph shot had been picked clean of feathers, then put in a brine bath to soak until morning.

Sarah had softened toward Daniel. They had begun talking again and now, they were pulling taffy in the kitchen, while Clay Jr. scraped a bowl of the last bit of chocolate icing Irene had made.

Lillian sat in a chair near the table, with one dozing baby in her lap, while she snapped beans in a large bowl. Reaching up, she brushed her hand across her throat, and looked around the kitchen. She turned to look left and right.

"Lillian, are you all right?" Irene asked. She emerged from the root cellar with a bowl of new potatoes to add to the beans Lillian was snapping.

"Oh, I'm fine. I just thought I felt a slight breeze, and wondered if someone had cracked a window, or if a door had been left open."

Joseph and Clayton could be heard stomping the snow and mud off their feet on the back porch. They opened the kitchen door in time to hear Irene call out, "Be sure to shut that door tight. We don't want anyone getting sick, do we?

"Mary, check to make sure no windows are open. It's easy to get chilled in this weather."

Clayton leaned down, and gave Lillian a firm kiss on the cheek before he pulled up a chair and lifted little Daniela Roberta from her lap.

Again, Lillian wiped at her neck and chin. "Clayton, I feel something tickling my face and neck. Is there a cobweb on my face?"

Clayton peered closely at his wife, squinting, while he examined her from chin to hairline.

"I don't see anything," he said, shaking his head.

"Look on my neck." She raised her chin and pulled down the neck of her bodice.

Irene went to help look, and both searched for whatever was causing the tickle.

"I don't seeing a thing, dear," Irene said, stepping back.

"Sorry, hon. Maybe it's a hair from one of the babies," Clayton suggested.

Lillian continued to hold her head high, and her stare grew intense. "How did that riddle go again?" Lillian asked slowly.

"You mean, 'look both high and low'?" Mary asked, while stamping out star-shaped cookies.

"No, the other part, about the eagle," her step-mother said.

"It isn't where the eagle flies, but where the eagle flew," Daniel answered, grinning. "I memorized it."

"Is the coffee hot?" Clayton asked, going to the stove.

"Oh, my, is it possible?" Lillian whispered hoarsely.

"Honey, what is it?" Clayton asked worriedly, seeing the strange look on Lillian's face.

"Daniel, say it again, what you memorized," Lillian said.

"It isn't where the eagle flies, but where the eagle flew," he repeated.

"Lillian, we've read that over and over. What's on your mind?"

"Get me a chair," she said firmly. "Put it against the wall by the stove."

"Honey, please..."

"No, please, get me a chair," she insisted.

Handing the baby to Mary, Clayton took the chair to where Lillian pointed. Once the chair was firmly against the wall, Lillian climbed on it, while Clayton held her hand to keep her balance.

She placed her free hand on the porcelain knob of the air vent on the stovepipe. After a few hard twists, and working it back and forth, it loosened, and she was able to unscrew it.

"Lillian, what does that have to do with the clue?" Sarah asked anxiously.

"Look at the stove pipe." Lillian pointed at the metal pipe she had only noticed moments ago while Clayton checked her neck.

"What?" Mary asked, peering up at the dark surface of the stove pipe.

"I see an eagle, but there're eagles all over this house," Sarah said.

"Yes, but this is the only eagle on the flue," Lillian said, smiling as she slipped a tiny rolled up paper out of the handle, and handed it to an astonished Sarah.

"Eagle f-l-e-w... eagle f-l-u-e... of course, it was right in front of our eyes and we just didn't get it. Dang, pardon me, ladies, darn, that was smart," Daniel said with a chuckle.

"How did you know?" Sarah asked in a hushed voice.

"I'm not sure. Something kept nagging at me. The woman wrote so well yet, I couldn't see her making it impossible to decipher her clues, since she had come by the gold so easily. Because of the wind, or whatever it was tickling me, I was holding my head up when I noticed the flue handle. I was thinking how pretty it is. Suddenly, I noticed the eagle."

"Yeah, the wind or... whatever it was," Clay echoed, causing Sarah and Mary to giggle.

"That was all it took? Sarah, what does it say?" Clayton asked, while everyone crowded around.

Sarah carefully straightened the tightly rolled message, peered at the tiny writing, and began to read aloud.

"When the sun shines through the
Eagle's eye
And reflects in the mirror within
It points to the final clue that
Will make a new world begin."

"Here we go again," Clay said, dejectedly. "We'll never figure out all that lady's clues. She don't want us to find it."

"I know where it is," Lillian said softly. "Irene, you do, too, don't you?"

Irene turned to gaze toward the hallway, and slowly nodded

"Do you think...?" Irene's voice trailed off. She rose and pushed open the double sliding doors to the hall.

"Bob, where are you going?" Joseph asked. He got up and followed her.

Everyone slowly trailed into the hallway, where Lillian stared at the stained glass inlay in the front door. The inlay decorating the two entry doors depicted a grassy meadow that rose toward the top of the pane. A large open-winged eagle adorned the upper pale-blue glass.

Lillian smiled, and Irene spoke. "If the sun was shining in from there," she explained, and pointed to the east, "early in the morning, it would come through here." She paused, and swept her arm from the door to the hallway.

"At one point, it would light the entire room. At some later time or other, it would directly hit *that*..." She pointed with a trembling finger to the mirror permanently fastened to the wall.

Lillian moved forward, her eyes shifting around the room. "There have been several times when I was dusting the living room, I had to shield my eyes from the reflection of the sun when I..." she stopped and went into the living room.

She walked around slowly, searching her memory for the exact spot where she stood when the sun blinded her. Going to the fireplace, she turned, looking left and right, and then back at the mirror.

"I was right about here." She stood to the right of the blazing fireplace.

The others grouped in the doorway, all looking back and forth from the mirror to where Lillian stood.

Daniel broke from the others, pulled on Clayton's sleeve, and said, "Let's check the bricks on the mantle."

Almost immediately, they all rushed to the fireplace and began checking the bricks and trim.

"He-e-ey," Clay cried, and looked at the others. "One of the bricks wiggled."

"Move son, let me see," Joseph said gently. "We don't want to destroy anything. If it's just dried mortar, we might have to scrape around the brick."

However, when he placed his fingers on the front and side of the brick, it slid out easily. He worked his hand into the opening, and felt around. He shook his head.

"I don't feel anything."

"Wait," Sarah said. She looked at Mary and her brother. "Remember when we found the picture of Aimee dressed as a man? I remarked how tiny she was, and how slim and delicate her hands were? Maybe..." she paused and grabbed Mary's hand. "Maybe, the opening was specially made for a little hand. Mary, you feel around in there."

"E-w-w-e-e!" Mary cried, her face puckered as if she were sucking on a lemon. "What if there're spiders or bugs in there? I don't think I can do it."

"I'll do it," Clay said, bouncing from foot to foot.

"Go ahead, little buddy." Daniel encouraged the boy, and moved the footstool over for Clay to stand on.

Clay took a deep breath, smiled at Daniel, and slowly inserted his hand into the hole. With his lips pinched and eyes squinted, he wiggled his fingers, and felt around.

"Work it around, feel everywhere," Sarah urged. "Stick your hand in farther."

Clay reach farther, and wormed his hand in deeper. Suddenly a smile illuminated his face.

"What is it, Clay? Say something," Mary squealed.

"It's a ring, I think," he said, and struggled to push his hand in even farther. "I got it."

He straightened up and gave a tug. Nothing happened. The boy grimaced, placed his free hand against the bricks, and with all the strength he could muster, he pulled. His face grew red, and a vein stood out on his forehead. A slight smile replaced his tight lips, and a twinkle appeared in his eyes. Then, with a grunt, a loud click could be heard.

Gasps and cries filled the room when the end of the fireplace swung outward, revealing a door just beside the fireplace.

"Oh, my gracious," Irene gasped.

They pushed the door open, and peered inside. There were shelves, and dozens of small boxes were stacked on each shelf. An old leather traveling bag, similar to the one Aimee had described as Abram's, sat against the back wall. One end of the shelf was dotted with wooden hooks, with dresses hung on them. A small armoire next to the leather bag was filled with lacey petticoats, fragile stockings, and shawls of the finest yarn. A tall mirror stood next to the armoire. The room seemed frozen in time.

The once chattering group stood paralyzed in silence, their eyes examining every inch of the room.

Sarah took small, faltering steps inside, and with a trembling hand, opened the carpet bag. With great care, she removed the contents. There were two dresses, simple, plain, and worn, several yellowed petticoats with little pockets sewn along the edge. There were four paper thin handkerchiefs, a pair of spectacles, plus a cheap, narrow silver band. Sarah removed a scuffed pair of high buttoned shoes, and two pairs of well-patched stockings.

Turning toward the others, a sob escaped, and tears streamed down her face.

"It's true," she gulped. "This is the proof her tragic story is really true."

Daniel was first to reach her. He enveloped her in his arms, held her close, gently stroking her hair.

"It's alright, Sarah, don't cry."

"I-t-t's j-j-ust..." she couldn't continue.

"I know. But it's what Aimee wanted, don't you see? It's the completion of her legacy. She's succeeded in passing on a good life to someone else, even when there was a time she didn't think she would be able to live one."

"H-h-how d-did you know what I was thinking?" She said against his shoulder.

"I know more about you than you think," he said, and pulled back so he could look into her eyes. "But not as much as I'd like."

"If this is the final clue, then where is it?" Clay whispered.

"There," Irene said.

She and Lillian looked at the space above the leather bag at the same time.

On the upper wall was a large sheet of parchment paper with a sketch of the herb garden and the fountain, with the tiny statues drawn in. At the top of the page were the words, *Garden of Gold*, and in the far right corner was a note.

> *There are two places in this world*
> *where I can be Aimee McKay.*
> *One is in this room*
> *And the other is in*
> *The Garden of Gold.*

"Does that mean what I think it does?" Clayton asked.

Daniel and Sarah gently fastened the leather strap of the traveling bag, stepped out of Aimee's secret room with the others, and stood quietly. Sarah pushed the brick door tightly closed. The click of the latch snapped loudly and the door locked. Joseph replaced the brick and stood among the silent family.

Suddenly, with a whoop, Lillian grabbed her shawl, swung it around her shoulders, and headed toward the kitchen, while the others raced for their coats and scarves. She was the first to step into the backyard.

It had started to snow again, turning the garden into a magic wonderland. The fountain had frozen over, and the little piles of snow on the tops of the dolphin and mermaids made the scene look like a world of sugar and frosting.

Approaching the statue of King Neptune, Lillian bent down, and dusted the falling flakes from his shoulder. Clayton came up beside her, took his knife, and began to scrape at the finish.

The discolored outer layer began to flake away, and the finish turned from a greenish gray to coppery bronze, and below the bronze, the metal became shiny yellow. He moved deeper into the garden, knelt down and scraped at the turtle that was now exposed since the herbs had died away. It, too, revealed a golden interior.

Lillian's knees grew weak and she sat down heavily on the nearby bench.

Suddenly the garden was filled with an icy breeze that danced around the garden, circling each individual. O-o-ohs and a-a-ahs filled the air. The otherworldly atmosphere was shattered by the demanding wails of twins who had been ignored long enough. Lillian shot to her feet at the first sound of the crying. And Daniel went to Sarah's side, while Irene hurried off to help Lillian with the twins.

Joseph looked at Clayton, who seemed to be in a daze.

"Deck the halls with boughs of holly," Mary sang. She and Clay began dancing in circles.

"Fa-la-la-la-la, la-la-la-la," Clay finished.

"'Tis the season to be jolly," Joseph joined in with his deep gravelly voice, waving his arms as if he was conducting a choir.

"Merry Christmas, Aimee," Sarah shouted. She threw her arms out wide, dancing in a circle. "And thank you for your wonderful gift. We'll be sure to pass it on to someone else."

Lillian and Irene returned to the garden, with the babies wrapped in wool blankets.

"Say what you will," Lillian said softly, and nuzzled the soft cheeks of her babies. "These are the best gifts of all. Aimee gave us a wondrous gift, but the good Lord gave us the best gift of all."

"Amen," Clayton said.

"Amen," the others chorused.

"Oh, mercy," Irene squealed, handing the baby she was carrying off to Mary. "I forgot all about the cake in the oven. I hope it's not burned."

Joseph laughed so hard he almost lost his balance.

"I have a feeling that gold isn't going to change things around here much," Clayton said, with a chuckle.

"Not when thousands of dollars' worth of gold takes a back seat to squawlin' babies, and an over-cooked cake," Joseph agreed.

"Or to the face of a pretty girl," Daniel added. Sarah blushed, Mary grinned, and Clay rolled his eyes.

"You know, I think Aimee must have known this, too. She found true love, discovered good friends, and had her family returned to her. We found good friends, Pa met Lillian, and Daniel found a family," Mary said softly.

"And I've discovered that having a yard full of gold don't warm a freezing behind," Joseph said through chattering teeth. "Can we be grateful inside, where it's warm?"

Clayton burst out laughing and Daniel joined him.

"You've got a point, Joe. Let's get inside," Daniel said, throwing his arm over Joe's shoulders.

They entered the kitchen, and Baby Joey and Daniela began to fret, but Irene was ready for them.

"You're gonna have to get your own coffee, gentlemen. The babies demands come first," she said.

Lillian took off to the bedroom to nurse little Joey. Irene took Daniela from Mary, and followed behind.

"I say we raise our cups to Miss Aimee McKay, and the treasure of babies, family, good friends, and her legacy, which we vow to pass forward. God bless Miss Aimee and the Legacy of Eagle Creek," Clayton toasted, and raised his cup toward the heavens.

"God bless Miss Aimee," the others chorused.

And a cool breeze danced happily throughout the house.

~ END ~

ABOUT THE AUTHOR

Bobbie Shafer is a native Texan living in Troup, Texas with her husband, Gordon. She is the mother of Connie, Kim, Cary, and Kelly; grandmother of Kandice, Josh, and Nellie; and cares for three goats, twelve cats, two dogs, and seventeen chickens.

Bobbie has published over 350 short stories and articles with various magazines in the past four years. Her first novel, *Loves Golden Dream* was released in October of 2011, from Dancing With Bear Publishing, and is Book One of the *Secrets of Eagle Creek Series*, and *Legacy of Eagle Creek* is Book Two.

Bobbie also has a story in the anthology, *The Latke Hound*, called *A Homemade Christmas*, available from Dancing With Bear Publishing.

Please purchase Bobbie's books at
www.dancingwithbearpublishing.com

You can find Bobbie at:

Website
www.BobbieShafer.com

Facebook
https://www.facebook.com/bobbie.shafer.3

Twitter
https://twitter.com/#!/BobbieShafer

LinkedIn
http://www.linkedin.com/pub/bobbie-

shafer/37/236/3b0

You can email Bobbie at bobbiejshafer@gmail.com

World Wide Who's Who Author Page Bobbie Shafer
Amazon Author Page Bobbie Shafer